Ju
F
G96   Gur, Motta.
         Azeet, paratrooper dog.

Temple Israel Library
Minneapolis, Minn.

———

Please sign your full name on the above card.

Return books promptly to the Library or Temple Office.

Fines will be charged for overdue books or for damage or loss of same.

AZEET, PARATROOPER DOG

AZEET, PARATROOPER DOG

by

General Motta Gur

THOMAS NELSON INC.

Nashville   New York

Copyright © 1972 by General Motta Gur

All rights reserved under International and Pan-American Conventions.
Published in Nashville, Tennessee, by Thomas Nelson Inc. and simulta-
neously in Toronto, Canada, by Thomas Nelson & Sons (Canada)
Limited. Manufactured in the United States of America.

First edition

Library of Congress Cataloging in Publication Data

Gur, Motta, date
    Azeet, paratrooper dog.
    Translation of Azit ha-kalbah ha-tsanhanit.
    SUMMARY: Recounts the exploits of an extraordinary German shep-
herd attached to an Israeli paratrooper unit patrolling the border.
                [1. Dogs—Stories.   2. Israel—Fiction]
I. Title.
PZ7.G9814Az   [Fic]   72-2918
    ISBN 0-8407-6252-6

CONTENTS

INTRODUCTION

The State of Israel became independent in 1948. It started its existence fighting the War of Liberation against its neighboring Arab states. In 1949, a formal state of war was replaced with an armistice.

But things didn't remain quiet very long. In the surrounding states, terrorists organized themselves into bands and set out on guerrilla missions to kill and destroy inside Israeli territory.

Zahal, the Israeli army, prepared itself to defend the borders, adopting fighting methods which suited the terrain and took into account the behavior of the enemy. Their techniques included the use of trained dogs who knew how to guard the settlements against the inroads of the terrorists and could pursue and track them down.

In those days I was an officer in a paratroop unit. As in any other army, the paratroopers were assigned to special tasks. One of these tasks was guarding the borders. We needed dogs very badly. We applied to the police force, which used trained dogs, and asked for as many as could be spared. An officer in the force told me that in Jerusalem there was a dog with unusual talents, and he recommended that I acquire her for Zahal.

I made the trip to Jerusalem, a city well known to me from the days of my own childhood, so that I was always happy to get back to it. The address was in one of the outer sections of town. I found it to be a three-story house, one of the older buildings in the neighborhood. I climbed the stairs to the third floor and found the name that had been written down for me on the slip of paper in my hand: *Dr. Harubi, Pediatrician.* I rang the doorbell and immediately heard a dog's growl.

"Open the door, Azeet," I heard from a pleasant voice on the other side of the door. The voice had no note of command in it.

I had never heard the name Azeet and was thinking of how unusual it sounded when a strong tap on the door handle opened the door wide.

I drew back. Standing before me was a large, beautiful German shepherd dog.

"Don't be afraid, my dear paratrooper," the voice said, and, to the dog: "Let our guest come in."

My eyes were still on Azeet. She turned around and grandly led the way into the interior of the apartment. I followed her, thoroughly captivated. Azeet paused by an armchair.

"Have a seat," Dr. Harubi said. "I have already

been notified by the police that you will be coming along. That is why I let Azeet do the honors. Happy to know you."

We shook hands and sat down. Dr. Harubi looked about forty; he was of medium height. His Hebrew was grammatically correct, but the accent had a peculiar European singsong. My host hardly gave me a chance to ask a single question about Azeet. I could see that he loved the dog with all his heart as he told me about her.

"I've always had a fondness for German shepherd dogs," he began. "When I was a boy in Germany we always had them at home, and I learned to love them and marvel at their wisdom. About a year and a half ago, a friend gave me Azeet as a gift; she was only a few weeks old. My friend told me that Azeet had a long pedigree and that her blood line had a reputation for bravery and extraordinarily well-developed senses, especially smell and tracking ability. I was very glad to have Azeet and began training her according to all the rules. When she was nine months old I sent her to the police for a training period, and in no time at all she was piling up all sorts of records. The police inspector suggested that I take time off from work and train along with Azeet, so that we might work together. I did, and I haven't been sorry for it.

"We did everything together—almost. I didn't jump hurdles, of course, but she and I spent many hours, day and night, doing tracking and stalking exercises. Azeet managed to track down lost persons, stolen clothing, special items—everything by smell, naturally. Soon we were in the thick of police action, and Azeet became the terror of thieves.

"We trained in this manner for about five months. Finally I had to go back to my own work, but we spend every weekend drilling, and once in a while the police call on us for a special assignment. We are always happy to oblige."

While Dr. Harubi was talking, Azeet kept moving around the room with quiet dignity, like a person too modest to stand by and listen to his praises. She was tall, with gray-black fur, and she had large eyes and teeth and a long pink tongue. Dr. Harubi proceeded to put her through her paces. She brought him a newspaper, handed me a bowl of fruit which she carried between her teeth, and closed the door—exactly as she was told to do. Her walk was easy—swift but majestic.

My excitement rose by the minute. I told Dr. Harubi why I had come—that we needed Azeet to protect the border.

The doctor agreed immediately, with not a moment's hesitation. But he made one condition —to join us. I asked Dr. Harubi if he had any objection to our training Azeet to parachute. "Of course not," he replied, "but not me. I'm too old."

We parted company as though we were old friends. By the end of the week, Dr. Harubi and Azeet reported for duty. Azeet passed the parachute course easily, special gear and all. As soon as she became accustomed to our unit we took her along on operational missions. To our delight, Azeet displayed extraordinary sensory powers. We kept demanding more and more of her. In a short time Azeet became part of our outfit and was regarded as Paratrooper Number One in the Corps.

This book tells the story of a few of Azeet's many exploits during her tour of duty with an Israeli paratroop unit. She was severely wounded in a border incident near Jerusalem and died at home shortly thereafter.

1. A RAID INTO SINAI

Even though Israel's War of Independence ended with an armistice in 1948, there has not been real peace on her borders. Rather, there has been guerrilla activity back and forth all these years.

Hundreds of thousands of Jews have streamed to Israel from all over the world, including the Arab states. Often, they came with no possessions. In Israel, many turned to farming and built settlements from one end of the land to the other, and along the borders. The Arab states tried to stop this work by setting up special armed units of men who crossed the border and attacked the settlements, causing damage to life and property. In this way they hoped to undermine the readiness of the people to settle in these new areas and to force Israel's population to remain hemmed in on all sides, in the interior.

Israelis couldn't put up with this situation. Army units didn't limit themselves to mere defense of the settlements. In turn, they too

1

crossed the borders and struck heavy blows against the bases of the infiltrators and the army camps which helped them. Many of these operations were carried out by the paratroops, with good results. When I was old enough to enlist, I became a paratrooper. I learned what it was that made the paratroopers such good fighters: they had a strong will to make good, they believed that their cause was just, and, above all, their training was tough, real tough.

We did most of our drilling at night. For hours on end we walked in patrol along the border, in the Negev desert and the northern hills. We learned to know and to love the land in the heat of summer and in the cold of winter, on moonlit nights and in thick darkness. At first the nights used to frighten us. But we learned that the night is a faithful friend and will never betray you.

We worked hard to train ourselves to keep our bearings in the Negev, particularly in learning how to find water holes, the only source of life in the dry desert. The Bedouins live only in the vicinity of these water holes, and any army which operates in the desert must know where they are to be found.

Our commander would split us paratroopers up into groups of three and charge us with finding water holes. In every hole we would leave a note. A few hours later other units would go out to find the same holes and bring the notes back, and that was how the commander could tell that we really did find all the holes we were claiming.

One day our commander called us together and gave us a difficult assignment: we were to raid an Egyptian encampment in Sinai. This was a camp from which saboteurs went forth to lay mines along the Negev roads. It was located not far from the water holes of Kadesh Barnea, where the tribes of Israel passed on their way from Egypt to the Promised Land.

Eight of us paratroopers set out. We carried a large amount of water with us. We knew that we had a long way ahead of us and if we couldn't make it back by daylight we would have to have water until the following night if we didn't find any. We studied the map closely to pinpoint the location of the water holes, and we took along ropes with which to let our canteens down and bring the water up.

The night was dark. The moon didn't show and the stars were hidden behind the clouds. We came down from the Negev hills and crossed the border. Around us were hillocks, small but steep and studded with sharp stones. On the hill at the border several paratroopers were posted with an officer, ready to come to our aid if anything unforeseen should happen.

The heat was suffocating. The clouds seemed to bar the passage of air. Our faces were streaked with sweat, and our tongues were dry. Our shirts stuck to our bodies. Suddenly the hum of a motor came from above us. Ours or the Egyptians'?

"Paratroopers? Aircraft here. Do you hear me? Over."

We breathed more easily. Our plane. We would use it to transmit messages to the rear. "Aircraft. Paratroopers here. We hear you well. How are we coming through? Over."

"Aircraft here. I hear you. Anything to report? Over."

"Paratroopers here. No, nothing. Everything's in order. Thanks a lot. Over."

The sound of the plane died away and we kept going, feeling much better. Somebody was looking out for us.

We came out of the hillock area and entered a broad valley. Here we stopped for a few minutes' rest and, from memory, went over the path we had taken so that we would know how to get back when our task was done. Each of us took a few sips of water and we went back into file. We could make better time on the flat ground, and our commander lengthened his pace.

The clouds moved apart a bit and starlight showed through. Then, as if from underground, a volley of shots came our way.

"Follow me!" shouted our commander. Without waiting we charged the enemy, as we had been taught, firing with all our weapons.

"I've been hit," Gili called out. "In the thigh."

We kept charging. The Egyptians didn't even have time to flee. All of them were hit.

The unit medic examined Gili. The wound wasn't serious; neither the bone nor the nerve had been hit. We helped the medic bandage Gili and gave him some water.

"Look here," said Gili to the commander. "Don't be held up on my account. You keep going to the camp and I'll go back myself. If I go with you, we'll be behind time and maybe won't even get to carry out the assignment. I remember the way back very well. You have nothing to worry about."

"Nonsense," the commander said. "We won't abandon a man in enemy territory. Come, we'll help you, and we'll do the job together."

"Okay, I will try," Gili said, getting to his feet.

We divided his gear among ourselves, leaving him only his Uzi gun. We kept going, but it was soon clear that we couldn't stick to the schedule. The commander called for a halt. "Well, Gili, I guess you're right. You can't go on—but you can't go back alone. Five of us will go ahead, and two will return with Gili. Who volunteers to go back?"

We were all taken aback. We wanted to keep going and take part in the action, but it wasn't proper to refuse to help a comrade.

The commander knew what was bothering us. "Okay. I see that you aren't keen about going back. I guess I'll have to decide." His eyes went from one man to the next until they rested on me. "You!" he said. His eyes moved on and paused on Adi. "You!"

His eyes went back to me. "You're in charge. You have matches and kerosine?"

We checked and replied that we had.

"Fine. Take the reserve communications unit

and start back. Try to stick to the trail we left. We'll be using it on our return. If you feel that you can't go on, get in touch with the plane and with us."

"Don't worry, sir," I replied.

"See you in time."

"Good luck," I said. We waited until their forms disappeared in the darkness, then turned around and began to retrace our steps. I went first, Gili behind me, and Adi last. Every now and then I looked back to see how Gili was doing and if I was going too fast for him. The wound must have hurt a lot, but he clamped his lips with his teeth and didn't complain even once.

We crossed the valley and moved on to the hillock area. Progress became more difficult. Gili's wound had opened and was bleeding. Our water supply was running low. We hardly drank, but Gili needed a lot of water to keep him going. Adi and I were now walking alongside Gili and supporting him. A glance at my watch showed me that time was passing without our being aware of it.

I tried to contact our commander, but the hillocks interfered and the distance was too great. We waited for the plane to come around again. Finally, I decided to move away from the trail and head for one of the water holes. I knew that this was a risky decision, for the others might not be able to find us then. But we had to find water for Gili. We could not split up, since there were only three of us, and I didn't want one person to go on alone. So we continued, supporting Gili and looking for a water hole. According to the map, there was one less than a mile away. And sure enough, after half an hour of painful walking we found it.

Bitter disappointment awaited us; the water hole was dry.

The next hole was about a mile and a half farther on. We decided to go there, even though Gili was barely able to walk. A big army would have had it easier, with helicopters, but we could get out of there only by walking. But how were we to do it, with our injured friend?

Again I tried to get in touch with the commander or the plane, but no reply came. Suddenly we heard explosions in the distance and bursts of light streaked through the darkness. The men were in action! This cheered us up. We were glad because they had done the job, and also because they might overtake us on their way back.

Gili slumped to the ground. "I can't keep going, fellows," he mumbled, fainting.

I figured that we weren't far from the water hole. I left Adi with Gili and set out, at a fast pace, to find it. But I couldn't locate it. Could we have made a mistake? How would we be able to let the rest of the group know where we were? I went back to Adi and the two of us tried to find a way out. Gili was conscious and feeling a little better, but his leg couldn't hold him. We tried carrying him, but the pain was too sharp and we had to let him rest.

We tried again getting in touch with the men or the plane. We got the matches and kerosine ready to mark the spot for the plane and called on the unit: "Aircraft. Paratroopers here! Aircraft. Paratroopers here. Over." Nothing came back. We were losing hope when it came: "Paratroopers. Aircraft here! Paratroopers. Aircraft here. Do you hear me? Over."

Adi quickly put the kerosine on fire.

"Paratroopers here. We hear you well. Can you see the fire we lit? Over."

"Aircraft here. Wait. I'm looking. Clouds in the way."

"Paratroopers here. Aircraft, you are almost directly above us. Can you see the fire? Over."

"Aircraft here. Can't see a thing. Clouds are low and I can't chance dropping below them. I must go on. The unit ahead has a wounded man and I must drop him a stretcher."

The hum of the motor faded away, and so did our hopes. If the other unit had a wounded man, it couldn't afford to go looking for us. We tried to contact the plane again. This time we were more fortunate.

"Aircraft? Paratroopers here. Can you drop us some water on your way back? Over."

"Aircraft here. I'll do my best. End."

We could do nothing but wait. Gili fell asleep. Adi and I stood watch in shifts of one hour each. The night was ending, and dawn would soon be coming. We looked around for a shady spot where we could place Gili. The desert sun can be murderous for a wounded man.

The clouds scattered, and a sheetlike white mist descended on the hillocks. A call came over the unit.

"Paratroopers, aircraft here. Light a fire. I'm dropping some water.

We quickly lit the can of kerosine. I took it to the top of a hill so that the plane could see it above the mist.

"Paratroopers, aircraft here! I see you. I'm coming in for a drop."

Suddenly the bulky shape of the plane came out of the sky, and two small parcels separated themselves from its wing.

"Aircraft, bull's eye! Over."

"Aircraft here. Listen closely. I have a message from your commander. You are to remain where you are until nightfall. We'll get you out then. Over."

Suddenly I thought of Azeet. She would be of great help in finding us. "Aircraft, paratroopers here. Can you bring Azeet with you? Over."

"Aircraft here. I hear you. We'll do it. We'll find you. End."

Adi and I ran quickly to the parcels and brought them in, together with their parachutes. In them we found water, food, and candy, and, most important, medication for Gili and instructions on how to use it. Our commander had thought of everything.

The day passed without incident. The heat was terrible, but we stayed in the shade and had plenty of water. Gili napped most of the time. He was weak, but the pain wasn't too bad. As it was getting dark, a call came over the unit:

"Paratroopers, this is Aircraft. Rescue unit, with Azeet, is moving in your direction. Light a fire to mark your location. Over."

"Aircraft, Paratroopers here. We hear you well. We are waiting at the same spot. We'll light a fire. End."

This was good news. I knew that the rescue unit would have a hard time finding its way among the hillocks. The men were experienced in night movements, but having Azeet would be a great help.

We prepared cans of kerosine and set them on the hillock. Time ticked by very slowly. Then we heard the call through the unit, "Paratroopers, Aircraft here. Don't light a fire. Egyptian forces are in the area. Our unit got back, but the Egyptians may still be looking for it. Don't show yourselves. End."

Our tension grew, and the time went by even more slowly. Adi and I kept watch, guns ready. The Egyptians might well get to us before our men did. Now I was doubly glad that Azeet was with the rescue unit. Otherwise, without a fire to guide the men, they would never find us. We heard shots in the distance. That could mean that the unit had made contact with the Egyptians. We were still wondering about it when I heard the panting of an animal, and the next instant the familiar figures of Azeet and Dr. Harubi came into view.

"Hey, Azeet!" I called out. "And how are you, Doc?" I shook hands with the doctor and patted Azeet at the same time.

"How I am?" repeated Dr. Harubi. "Don't ask. If it weren't for Azeet, we would never have found you. She led us to you like Moses led our fathers to Mount Sinai."

Others came up, our commander among them. "Glad you held out," he said, shaking hands with all of us. "Let's get going. I'll fill you fellows in on what happened."

Four paratroopers set a stretcher on the ground. The unit medic examined Gili, gave him an injection, and attached a bottle of plasma to his arm. The four picked up Gili on the stretcher and we all left.

"Let me tell you what happened," Dr. Harubi whispered to me. "The commander set out with the unit along the trail, but you fellows moved off when you went to look for water. All the hillocks look the same, and if it hadn't been for Azeet's nose, our feet wouldn't have led us here. She always kept dragging us back to your tracks. Then we got word from the plane about the Egyptian force in the area. This meant that you couldn't light a fire to guide us. Just to make sure, the commander sent a decoy unit to lead the Egyptians away from you. The shots we've just heard were probably fired by that unit. We've also sent planes to the area. But you should have seen Azeet when she came on your scent. She pulled like crazy."

I gave Azeet another pat on the back.

The commander then told me that the raid on the saboteur camp had gone off according to plan. All those who were responsible for mining the Negev roads had been hit. Our wounded man had been transferred to the hospital and was resting comfortably. At daybreak we came to the hillock where we had parted company on the previous day. There we joined up with the decoy unit. The men had driven the Egyptians off without suffering a scratch. Everyone had words of praise for Azeet.

Gili was taken to the hospital and we went on to our camp.

On the following day our commander sent a letter of thanks to Dr. Harubi and Azeet. It said: "It is our honor and privilege to accept you in the paratroop unit."

To the letter the commander attached the red beret of the paratroopers.

2. RESCUE MISSION IN THE JUDEAN DESERT

Anyone who has read the Bible knows of the Judean Desert. This region has always attracted many Jews. Though empty and desolate, it has a special atmosphere—a certain air of holiness.

The Prophets of Israel wandered through this desert to be alone with God and with themselves. Here the Maccabees found hiding places where they could gather their forces for future battles against the Greeks. Bar-Kochba and the Zealots fought the Romans here. And in the fortress of Masada, near the Dead Sea, a handful of heroes held many Roman legions at bay for three years.

Young people have always loved to hike in the Judean Desert. Though parched and barren, its scenery is breathtakingly beautiful.

After the War of Independence and the birth of the State of Israel, large stretches of the Judean Desert were outside Israeli borders. It was forbidden to go there, for the area was in Jordanian territory. Still, every now and then lovers of nature or of history, unwilling to go along with this separation, managed to pay a visit there.

15

One day we were told that two young people, Homi and Ruthie, had gone for a stroll into the desert and that nothing had been heard from them for two days. Homi and Ruthie were paratroopers; both were known for their love for the desert and their enjoyment of hiking. Our Foreign Ministry asked the Jordanians whether they were holding the two. When the Jordanians replied that they weren't we grew worried, thinking that they might have fallen into the hands of unfriendly Bedouins.

Our paratroop company received orders to go out to the desert and comb it from one end to the other. We were hopeful that the two were still in Israeli territory and had not crossed the border by mistake. We split up into three units and began to comb the desert systematically. The units left at dawn to check all the gullies and mountain crags.

We drew up a plan for each day's operations. In the Judean Desert you can't go ahead without a plan. Some deserts have level sand, where you can move in any direction, but the Judean Desert is not one of them. This is a desert of tall mountains and deep gullies. In order to move along here, you must select a march route planned beforehand, either along the gullies or atop the ridges, otherwise you will come up against impassable crags and clefts.

In the morning, after the units had gone out for the combing operation, I boarded a Piper at the Beersheba airfield and went up to search the area from above. From the plane it was possible to scan large stretches and examine areas inaccessible on foot. The plane had a communications instrument by which I kept in touch with the company units below. Around noon a Dakota plane appeared, with water tanks ready to be parachuted down to the searchers. The paratroopers below lit a smoke candle to mark their location, and the tanks came floating down to them. Later, in the evening, I met with the unit leaders to plan the next day's operations. We knew that we would have to step up the pace of the search if we wanted to reach Homi and Ruthie in time to find them still alive.

At dawn on the third day the units went out again, and I went up in the plane with Ori, the Piper's pilot. I got in touch with the unit leaders below, then went on to scout the area which I had marked out for myself for that morning. The gorges were so deep that we had to fly through the gullies, with walls of solid rock rising on either side of us. At times we dived so low that we had trouble pulling up again. Then we would fly above the crags, but so close to them that only a few yards separated us from them. Ori was really something; in order to find Homi and Ruthie he risked his own life—and mine, of course—and the plane, many times.

We found nothing. The dives and climbs made me a little sick. It seemed that the whole world was dancing around me. Ori obligingly climbed higher. I opened the window a crack and let the cold air hit my face, then opened my mouth wide and gulped it in, at the same time loosening my belt. Slowly I began to feel better, and we went on with our search. We were now some twenty kilometers ahead of the paratroopers below. The region was pockmarked with many caves. From my studies in history I knew that the Judean Desert had large caves which people had used for refuge in the past.

"Let's go down and see if we can spot anything near the caves," I said to Ori.

Ori glanced at the map of the area.

"It's fine with me," he said, "but you should know that we're just about at the border. We're bound to cross over into Jordanian territory as we circle."

"Go ahead," I said. "We have no choice. We must try. Dive down."

Ori set the plane for the dive and went down into the gullies. There was no sign of anything. I studied the area; no Bedouin encampments were to be seen. "Try on the other side of the border," I suggested.

"On your responsibility," said Ori, bringing the Piper around for another circle.

I scanned the area, somewhat nervously. If word got back to the army that we had crossed the border without permission, we would be in trouble—but good.

Suddenly I caught my breath. Down below, near one of the clefts, I spotted a paratrooper's knapsack. I pointed it out to Ori. "Drop down as low as you can," I said, but Ori already had the Piper's nose pointing straight at the knapsack.

We felt sure that the knapsack belonged to one of the two lost paratroopers, which meant that they couldn't be far away. But how could we get to them? No vehicle could make it to the spot, and there was no landing room for a paratroop force. The company units were still twenty kilometers away, and advance in this region was extremely slow and difficult.

"Azeet!" The thought flashed through my mind. We would parachute Azeet down and she would find the couple.

We passed the spot back and forth to see if we could spot anything else. Then Ori put the Piper into a climb and we streaked back to Beersheba. As soon as we touched ground I phoned Dr. Harubi in Jerusalem. When I told him the story, he said, "Of course! Tell me what to do."

"Get to the landing strip near Bet Hakerem," I told him. "I'm sending a Piper right away to bring you to the paratroop base."

I put in a call to the base. "Hold up the Dakota and get a parachute ready for a dog. We have to drop a dog in the desert."

Next I got in touch with the commanders of Homi's and Ruthie's units. "I want you to find something of their personal belongings—clothes, if you have them. Take it to the Dakota Flight. We need it for the dog that will be out looking for them."

I then phoned my own commander, explained the situation, and asked for a small communications instrument, a water canteen, and stimulant pills—all to be tied to Azeet.

The paratroop base went into speedy action. The needed equipment was collected, as well as blankets and warm clothing, food, and water. The Air Force dispatched a Piper to Jerusalem to pick up Dr. Harubi and Azeet. At the jet base several combat planes were prepared to accompany the Dakota and protect it as it flew beyond the border. Other combat planes were put on alert, in case the Jordanians tried to interfere with the rescue operation.

Ori and I went back to our plane and took off for the desert. Our communications code word was "Yair," the name of the Masada hero. I contacted all the units in the area.

"Yair posts! This is Yair. Do you hear me? Over."

"Yair A here. We hear you. Over."

"Yair B here. We hear you. Over."

"Yair C here. We hear you. Over."

"This is Yair. We have found signs at Point C. Get there as fast as possible. Over."

All the units confirmed the order.

The voice of the Dakota pilot came through the instrument: "This is Diamond. Am approaching the area. Over."

"I have you," Ori replied. "I'll show you the spot. Over."

As Dr. Harubi told me later, Azeet crouched in the aisle between the seats of the Dakota. Two strips from shirts belonging to Homi and Ruthie were tied around her neck, to keep her smelling their scent. Strapped to her back was a small communications instrument by which Dr. Harubi could give her instructions and which Homi and Ruthie might use later. A flat water canteen was attached to her belly, along with a special case containing a sharp knife, matches, and medicines.

All this gear was topped with the harness of the automatic parachute. One of its straps was already hooked on to the steel wire in the plane. As Azeet made the jump from the plane, this strap would open the parachute.

The parachute had another special feature—a release mechanism which would free Azeet from it as soon as she hit the ground. Otherwise the parachute would drag behind her all the time, and a strong wind could fill it and pull the dog along in the wrong direction.

Dr. Harubi sat near Azeet and communicated with her through the instrument, to get her used to it. Azeet caught on immediately. Every once in a while Dr. Harubi put the strips of the shirts close to her nose, to remind her of the scent.

We reached the target area. I chose a more or less convenient spot and waited for the Dakota. When I saw it coming I signaled to Ori to head down. I opened the window, took out a red smoke grenade, and pulled the pin. As we reached the selected spot I tossed the grenade out of the window. The plane climbed immediately.

"Do you see the smoke grenade?" Ori called to the Dakota.

"I see it. Ready for paradropping."

Arik, the Dakota's pilot, swung his craft around in order to come in against the wind. The red smoke indicated an easterly wind, and Arik headed west.

A bell rang in the Dakota. Adi and Nir, the dispatchers, stood on either side of Azeet and called, "Hear now!"—the signal to paratroopers before the jump.

Azeet rose easily to her feet. Adi and Nir checked the harness and the release mechanism to make sure that everything was in good order. Adi motioned to Gil, the copilot, and Arik leveled the plane and glanced at the gauges to make sure that he was at the proper altitude— eight hundred feet above the ground. Adi and Nir kept their eyes on the framehead and waited for the red light. Arik pressed a button, and the red light went on.

"Ready!" Adi and Nir called out, leading Azeet to the door. The two men were tied to the plane with safety belts. They held the door open with one hand and grasped the harness of Azeet's parachute with the other.

The Dakota came up fast to the jump area. From the Piper we could easily see Azeet in the exit doorway.

Arik pressed a button. The light on the framehead turned green.

"Jump!" yelled Adi and Nir, giving Azeet a gentle shove forward.

The shove wasn't needed. Azeet dived into the open air as though she were jumping into a swimming pool. We saw her feet wiggle a bit, and at once the parachute opened. Azeet settled into the

harness and began floating downward, gently and calmly.

Adi and Nir hauled in the strap which had opened the parachute and remained in the doorway to watch Azeet. Dr. Harubi lay prone on the floor, his chin almost over the sill, as he watched his dog and kept murmuring words of endearment to her.

The easterly wind was light, and the parachute floated downward with hardly any shifting at all. Azeet craned her head a bit to get a good look at the ground that was coming up to meet her. We came closer in the Piper and were happy to see that she was about to land on a good spot. She touched earth on all fours. The release mechanism worked perfectly; the parachute was detached from her in a split second.

Azeet shook herself and scanned the area. Dr. Harubi called to her through the instrument, "Azeet—search!"

The dog began trotting around the spot in ever-widening circles, keeping her head low. The circles grew until we saw that she was at the brink of the crag below which the knapsack was lying. Would she find it?

From the plane it was impossible to detect any footprints. The area around the crag resembled a sheet of rock. The crag itself seemed so steep that no one could possibly climb along its face without ropes.

Azeet stopped suddenly and raised her head. Dr. Harubi understood that she had sensed something. "Azeet—search!" he again said, through the instrument.

Azeet lowered her head again and began moving along the crag. Her steps became more hurried. But why was she drawing away from the knapsack?

"Good Azeet," Dr. Harubi called to her. "Search!"

Azeet was certainly on the trail of something. Her movements were swift and sure—but she kept moving away from the knapsack.

Suddenly she jumped into a small cleft and disappeared from view.

A cave? Could Homi and Ruthie have gone into a cave and let their knapsack slip down to the gully below, or had someone taken it and let it drop?

We had the answer when Azeet suddenly appeared near the knapsack, as though she had emerged from the wall. She stopped and sniffed at the knapsack from all sides. We understood that some kind of tunnel led down from the crag to the gully. That was how Azeet got there—and so probably had Homi and Ruthie.

But where were they now? We kept flying above the point in tight circles so that we would not lose sight of Azeet. The Dakota circled above us. Dr. Harubi still lay near the door and kept talking to the dog.

Azeet began moving along the slope of the gully, leaping among the boulders like a goat. Suddenly she disappeared again. We waited for her to show herself again, but, as we found out later, she was too busy. She had found Homi and Ruthie.

The two were lying in a cave, bound hand and foot, gagged and helpless. Their attackers had taken their shoes and all their possessions and had tied their feet to a jutting rock. Fortunately it was cool inside the cave, but being without food or water for several days had made them faint and sleepy.

They first knew of Azeet's presence when Homi felt something moist licking his face. He opened his eyes. The sight of the big dog frightened him, but as soon as he heard Dr. Harubi's voice coming through the instrument he understood that she was there to help them. Homi shook Ruthie awake.

Azeet barked loudly—once, twice. Up in the Dakota, Dr. Harubi gave a shout of delight. This was Azeet's way of saying "Mission accomplished."

"She has found them," Dr. Harubi said to Adi and Nir. He turned to the microphone. "Homi—there's food and water and other things attached to Azeet. Do you hear me?"

Homi did, but he couldn't reply—until Azeet's teeth clamped the gag and tore it out of his mouth. As Homi moved his jaw around because it was stiff, Azeet repeated the performance with Ruthie.

Homi bent toward the instrument. "I hear

you," he said, his weak voice barely audible. "Do you hear me?"

We were overjoyed. From the Dakota came Dr. Harubi's voice: "Is Ruthie with you?"

"Yes, we're both here. Thanks for the hairy angel you sent us."

The "angel" was busy with the ropes that tied Homi's hands and feet. One after another the knots came undone. Homi's hands felt Azeet's body and found the case with the knife. It took no more than a few strokes to set Ruthie free. Homi unscrewed the canteen, gave Ruthie a few sips of water, and drank some himself, then gave the rest to Azeet. The dog lay on the floor of the cave, panting lightly, and gazed curiously at the people she had found.

"We're coming out right away," said Homi into the instrument. "Just as soon as our muscles begin working again."

Azeet waited until the two had flexed their muscles enough to restore circulation, then went out with them into the open. We saw Homi and Ruthie crawling up the face of the crag. They didn't dare wave to us; one bad move would have sent them plunging down into the gully. Azeet led the way and they followed her into the tunnel. A few minutes later we saw them emerge in the cleft.

"Hear now," came Dr. Harubi's voice. "We are dropping supplies for you from the Dakota." Arik swung the plane around as Adi and Nir prepared to drop the supplies from a very low altitude, without parachute.

"Hear now!" Arik pressed the button for red and let the craft drop a bit. Adi and Nir brought the parcels to the exit.

The gauge showed twenty meters. Arik pressed the button. As the green light showed, Adi and Nir pushed the packages out of the plane. They hit the ground with a dull thud and rolled on a bit. Azeet streaked forward to stop them, but they were right on target.

"You have there everything you need," came Dr. Harubi's voice. "Food and weapons. Don't worry. The paratroopers will be here in a few hours. The Air Force has planes aloft to protect you. You're perfectly safe."

"Thanks," replied Homi. "We'll be fine."

"Another thing," went on Dr. Harubi. "In the parcels you'll find cans of meat, for Azeet. Let her eat her fill. She deserves it."

3. AZEET BECOMES A FROGMAN

The day was cloudy. A light rain sprayed the slopes of Mount Carmel. Adam and Hillel, Navy Corpsmen, were in their positions atop the Carmel, peering through their powerful binoculars for some sign of approaching enemy ships out in the murky waters.

Karen, a Navy Corpswoman, was doing the same—but deep in a cellar. She sat in front of the radar screen and kept track of the ships at sea. The underground chamber was dark and full of people. Men and women of the Navy Corps sat in front of the screens. Officers stood by the telephones and the radio, ready to receive and pass on orders. Karen's screen showed nothing new. The green ray of light, moving clockwise around the screen, flashed across the shore outlined on it, as well as a number of ships on the water. Karen checked all the signs to make sure that no new ship had come into the picture. If she did find such a sign, she would have to let the war room of the Navy Corps command know about it at once.

Tali's post was at the huge board, on which were drawn the Israeli coastline and the entire Mediterranean Sea. Toy ships were set on the board as markers to show the position of ships according to the signs picked up on the radar screen. In Tali's hand was a long pointer, tipped with a magnet. Each time Karen reported any change on the radar screen, Tali would use the pointer to move the ship marker accordingly.

The Navy commanders were at the battery of telephones and radio instruments, through which they gave orders to the warships at sea.

In another cellar, this one belonging to the Air Corps, Rotam kept her eyes glued to her radar screen. Her job was to follow the flight of aircraft aloft and to spot at once any strange plane entering Israel's air space. A telephone at her elbow kept her in touch with Tali and Karen, and all news was quickly passed on to Enat, at Staff Headquarters, for transmission to the Navy war room and the Israel Defence Forces General Staff.

A new point appeared on the radar screen. Rotam and Karen spotted it at the same time. Karen immediately informed the Navy war room about it, while Tali placed a new toy ship on the board in front of her. The Navy commander ordered all warships to be on the alert. Torpedo boats were sent toward the unidentified ship.

Rotam passed the information on to Air Corps

Headquarters. The Corps commander ordered a Mirage squadron to stand by, ready for takeoff. Two planes were sent up to find the ship and identify it. The radar screen showed the strange vessel to be far offshore, so that there was as yet no danger of its doing any damage to Haifa itself.

Enat let the General Staff know about these preparations. All the steps taken by the Navy and Air Corps were approved. The chief-of-staff ordered that the vessel be attacked immediately if it was identified as an enemy ship.

From their lookout point, Adam and Hillel could see the torpedo boats streaking out into the open sea. Their binoculars also showed that the ship was an Egyptian missile-carrying warship.

Suddenly balls of fire were seen on the deck of the Egyptian craft.

"Look!" shouted Adam excitedly. "Our boys are hitting it."

Overhead came the buzzing of the Mirages. Adam and Hillel looked up, but the planes had disappeared into the clouds. The two returned to their posts just in time to see something flying in the air. "They're firing missiles!" Hillel cried. "Inform the war room at once!"

As Adam was transmitting the news to Tali, a huge column of water rose out in the sea, followed by a thunderous explosion. One missile, then another, blew up in the water.

The Navy commander nodded in satisfaction. The missiles were far off the mark. The commander of the Egyptian warship had evidently seen the torpedo boats streaking toward his vessel and decided to fire his missiles and get away.

But it was too late. No sooner had the two missiles left the deck than torpedoes came straight at the enemy vessel from all three boats. Adam and Hillel saw three explosions shake the Egyptian warship. A few minutes later it sank below the surface and disappeared.

The torpedo boats kept circling around on the water. They picked up any Egyptian sailors who were able to escape from the ship before it went to the bottom. The Mirages zoomed above the spot, then banked low, tilting their wings up and down in a sign of congratulations to the Navy boats: "Good job!"

At the staff headquarters it was decided not to let the attack on Haifa go by without a reply of some sort. A counterattack was ordered on the Egyptian fleet. On that same night, a force of frogmen was sent, under Gadi's command, to attack the military harbor in Alexandria, where many Egyptian warships were lying at anchor. The frogmen were taken there in a submarine. In the course of their operations, the frogmen sank many ships and damaged others, but they were unable to get back to the submarine which was to take them home. In the daytime the frogmen hid in small caves at the edge of the shore and waited for nightfall, when the submarine was to approach the harbor and pick them up. But the submarine commander couldn't tell what was happening inside the harbor, nor did he dare draw near. Following the attack on the Egyptian warships, the harbor was full of enemy boats.

The submarine returned to deep water. The commander couldn't make contact with the home base in Israel because his signals could be intercepted by the enemy. But the home base on the other hand could keep sending messages to the ships at sea, repeating them over and over to make sure that they were received.

When the Navy Corps commander found that the submarine hadn't come back he became worried about its fate, and the fate of the frogmen. He knew that the operation had been successful and that many Egyptian ships had been put out of action, but he was concerned about his men and wanted to do everything possible to get them home. He called in his staff officers. After talking the situation over, they decided that in the evening they would send out a helicopter with more men to the submarine.

I suggested that they take Azeet along to help in the search.

The Air Corps let the Navy have a large "Super Ferlon" helicopter, a three-motored craft capable of flying far out to sea. Even if one engine should conk out, this "chopper" could still keep going.

A light helicopter brought Dr. Harubi and Azeet to the naval base. When they got there, they found the men ready to board the Super Ferlon as soon as they would receive final instructions from Hami, the helicopter's pilot.

Dr. Harubi was handed a submachine gun. Both he and Azeet wore life belts.

Dani, the commander of the unit, told his men,

"We are facing a tough task. We have to rescue our men. They carried out a very dangerous assignment in Alexandria Harbor yesterday. Because they fulfilled their task so well, they couldn't get to the submarine and are probably still on shore. The Egyptians are no doubt looking for them everywhere. We have no information as to where our men are, and we are taking along Azeet to help us find their tracks.

"Hami's helicopter will take us to the submarine. Its commander will be told where to meet us. At exactly five thirty-two he will surface the sub, for a few moments only. We'll jump down from the helicopter into the water and swim to the submarine, which will take us on, submerge, and head underwater for Alexandria. In the darkness the sub will let us out, together with our rubber boats, and we'll row to the beach and begin looking for Gadi and his men. Strict silence will be observed during the entire operation. Any questions?"

Everything was clear.

Hami started the motors and the overhead rotor began swishing. The men boarded the craft. Azeet leaped into her seat as though she had been flying in a helicopter all her life. The technician closed the door and signaled to Hami that everything was in order.

The Super Ferlon lifted easily off the ground. The hour was 4 P.M.

Hami got in touch with Rotam in the Air Corps and told her that he was on his way. Rotam was very excited; after all, Hami was her cousin.

The Navy Corps commander radioed an order to Ori, commander of the submarine:

"Helicopter will land at five thirty-two P.M. at Point D. Take its men aboard and proceed on rescue operation of frogmen force."

Ori also became very excited when he got the order. He was glad to have the opportunity to help the frogmen, some of whom were old friends. He bent over the map on the table in his room. He located Point D, took a ruler and a compass, and plotted his own location to see in what direction and at what speed he should proceed in order to get to the point on time. They could not afford to lose a minute. As soon as the course was plotted, Ori gave an order:

"All engines forward. Azimuth seventy-six degrees!"

The chief engineer repeated the order from the engine room, "All engines forward."

From his station, the helmsman called out, "Azimuth seventy-six degrees!"

Ori called his officers together. He revealed the plan and told each man what he was to do. Everything was clear. The submarine was on its way to the meeting point.

In the helicopter, the men were treated to a surprise. A pretty girl soldier walked out of the pilot's cabin. She was carrying a trayful of sandwiches. Tami, a secretary at the helicopter base, had been determined to go on the flight and help the men. Hami finally had given in and had allowed her to board the helicopter secretly. Now she was acting as a stewardess. Dani was especially happy. He had met Tami in the course of joint training and the two had become very friendly. Tami came up to Dani and kissed him on the forehead, as all the others grinned. Dani blushed and crammed his mouth full of sandwich to cover up his confusion.

After the sandwiches came fruit juice and cookies. The men's spirits rose. Azeet got her share of everything, besides being stroked by everyone aboard. But the dog kept her eyes on Dr. Harubi, as if trying to read on his face what it was that she would have to do.

Dr. Harubi really had a problem—he had never been on combat duty at sea, and now he had to get Azeet used to taking orders from Dani.

Dani's love for dogs helped quite a bit. At the first touch of his hand Azeet knew that he was good friend.

"Azeet, shake hands with Dani," ordered Dr. Harubi.

Azeet extended her right paw.

"Azeet, let Dani feed you."

Azeet turned to Dani's outstretched hand. Her upbringing and training made her hesitate. She looked again at Dr. Harubi, as if asking, "May I, really?"

"Let Dani feed you," repeated the doctor.

Azeet lifted her long nose and bit off a piece of a cookie.

"Good girl!" Dani stroked Azeet's head, and she didn't move away. Now that Dr. Harubi had given her orders, she was ready to go along all the way.

Dr. Harubi turned to Dani. "Try giving her a few orders, in my presence."

The other men kept their eyes intent on the training lesson.

"Come to me, Azeet!" whispered Dani.

Azeet looked questioningly at Dr. Harubi. "Go, Azeet," the doctor said, pointing to Dani.

The dog arose slowly and came close to Dani.

"Good girl!" the doctor encouraged her, patting her on the back.

"Good girl!" repeated Dani, stroking her head.

Step by step, Azeet was made to understand that she was to do everything that Dani would ask of her.

A few of the men now took a nap. The tense preparations for their task had worn them out. Silence came over the helicopter. Only Tami came in every few minutes to ask if anyone wanted to eat or drink. But all the men had eaten and drunk their fill. They leaned back against the walls of the craft and chewed gum. Dani spread the map and photographs of Alexandria Harbor out on the floor and went over the operations that he and his men were to carry out.

Azeet lay quietly, her head on her forelegs, eyes closed.

Dr. Harubi went over to Tami. "If you can get Azeet some water, I'll be grateful to you."

"Sure thing," Tami replied. She took an old pilot's hat and, with Dr. Harubi's help, filled it with water from one of the containers and offered it to the dog.

Azeet drank thirstily. The candy and sweet cookies had parched her tongue.

The hour for the meeting was approaching. Hami looked down into the growing darkness. Nir, his copilot, was busily studying their route on the map—a black line with arrows, broken into sections, with the exact flying time for each.

The sea was smooth, shimmering with small steady ripples which kept the water moving. Not a single ship was to be seen on the horizon.

Hami pressed a button. A sharp jangle aroused the drowsy men. Azeet raised her head at the new sound. The men settled back in their seats. Tami came to the doorway. "Anyone want anything to drink?"

"No, thanks."

The men checked their life belts. Dr. Harubi made sure that Azeet's was tightly fastened.

The mechanic checked the exit door; it opened

easily. He signaled to Hami over the intercom that everything was ready. Hami pressed the button once more.

"Stand by!" Hami called back to the men. Azeet stood between Dr. Harubi and Dani.

Below them the water sped by swiftly. Hami and Nir checked their watches. In another minute the submarine was due to surface.

Suddenly, almost directly below the helicopter, the water parted and a long, slim black body rose slowly. White flecks of foam skipped off the deck of the submarine as it came gracefully out of the sea.

Hami set the helicopter in a circle above the submarine and called into the microphone,

"Submarine, this is Helicopter. I am lowering the men and the dog."

The reply came at once. "Helicopter, this is Submarine. All set. Carry on immediately."

Hami pressed the button.

"Jump!" cried Dani. He plunged down first, with Azeet and Dr. Harubi at his side. In a few seconds all the men were in the water. Tami leaned out of the exit and waved to them. Dani waved back and threw her a kiss.

"Good luck!" shouted Tami, and the technician closed the door.

Several sailors came out on deck with ropes and life belts. They sent the belts skimming into the water. The men grabbed them and were pulled up to the deck.

Azeet watched the others and did exactly what

they did. She dived under the safety ring that was thrown to her, then came up inside it. The sailors towed her up. All this took but a few moments.

"Stand by for submerging!" ordered Ori from his position at the periscope, which he kept turning tensely in all directions to make sure that the submarine was not being observed.

All hatches were now down, and the submarine began to descend. From the helicopter Hami, Nir, and Tami watched the sub being swallowed up by the depths of the sea.

"Back we go," muttered Hami, turning the helicopter back to base.

Inside the submarine there was action at fever pitch. The first thing to do was to get away from the spot—and fast, in case someone had caught sight of the helicopter. Ori pressed the alarm bell for full dive, and its shrill sound cut through the submarine.

"All engines forward! Azimuth two hundred fifty-six degrees!"

"All hatches closed!" came the message to Ori in the control room.

"Fill the main tank with water," ordered Ori. "Dive at ordinary angle," he added, his eyes moving to the depth gauge.

The compressed air in the tank whistled as it emptied into the water outside and the water came pouring into the tank. Everyone had his eyes fixed on the control board and the gauges showing the course of the dive. The sub was now entirely submerged.

"Snorkel out," said Ori. He wanted to spare the electrical batteries and to keep the Diesel engines going; the snorkel supplied these engines with the air they had to have.

Reports kept coming to the control room from all over the submarine. Everything was going along well; it had been a perfect dive.

Mula, the officer in charge of the shift, took Ori's place to allow the sub's commander to talk with Dani. Ori told Dani what had happened the night before, and Dani told Ori all the latest news from the other battlefronts. One of the sailors brought them coffee, and the two men put their minds to the task facing them.

There were two ways to carry out the operation. Ori could bring the sub to the surface a long distance away from the port and let Dani and his men go on in their rubber boats. Having the boats along would make it possible to take back any of Gadi's men who might have been wounded.

The other way was to proceed as frogmen. The sub would remain below the surface, and Dani's men, with all their equipment, would get to the port by swimming, on and under the water. This way the sub would avoid running the risk of being seen by the Egyptian guards.

After a long discussion Ori and Dani decided on a combination course. Off Alexandria Harbor there were hulks of many ships which had gone up on the reefs and remained stuck there. Once the frogmen reached one of the hulks, as close to the port as possible, two of them would swim out to check the area. If no patrol boats were around, the sub would surface and tie up at the hulk, which would act as interference for the Egyptian radar. The Egyptians would be unable to detect the sub. The rest of the men would then go out with the rubber boats. As an alternative, if Egyptian patrols were around when the frogmen reached the wrecks, the sub would remain below the surface and the men would proceed by swimming.

Dani went back to his men and explained the plan to them. They decided on the order for leaving the submarine. Azeet would go first, with Dani and Moishele. Ori called for diving equipment for Azeet—air tanks on her back and a diving helmet fitted to her head.

"Let the helmet stay on her head for a few minutes," said Dani. "That way she'll get used to breathing through it."

Then a serious question came up: If Azeet wore the helmet all the time, would her sense of smell be able to work?

It was decided that Azeet would be tied to Dani by rope. Once they surfaced, Dani would remove the helmet. If they had to go under again, he would replace the helmet and signal to Azeet to dive. Dr. Harubi assured Dani that Azeet would understand the operation after the first time or two it was practiced.

Ori glanced at the gauge and went over to the map table. Mula gave him the details of the sub's progress, and together they pinpointed its location.

"Stand by to rise to snorkel level!" Ori ordered. The frogmen checked their gauges and apparatus. Reports kept coming in that everything was in order.

Dani and his men ate some chocolate and drank hot tea. Azeet had milk. It isn't advisable to eat a heavy meal before a hard swim.

From the scanning room came word that no large ship could be seen in the immediate vicinity. Now it was necessary to take a look through the periscope to make sure that no patrol boats were around.

"Rise to surface level!" ordered Ori, his eyes on the depth gauge.

The sub began to rise at a steep angle. The gauge dials showed 50 feet—40 feet—30 feet—20 feet—that was it!

"Check by periscope!" Ori called. He went over to the large periscope which had been thrust out above the water by pressure.

No one spoke. Tense but calm, all the men followed Ori's movements. He wasn't using the radar, because the waves it would send out in the air might be detected by the Egyptian radar.

"I see the hulk of one ship on the reef," Ori said. Mula marked its location on the map.

"Azimuth one hundred eighty degrees. All engines slow!" ordered Ori.

"All engines slow," came the repeat from the engine room. The motor slowed down.

"One hundred eighty degrees," called back the helmsman, giving the rudder an expert turn.

Dani and Ori shook hands.

Dani went back to the spot where Azeet, with her gear of tanks and helmet, was standing. "Come on, old girl," he said.

Dr. Harubi patted his dog on the head. "Go ahead, Azeet," he said.

Dani and Azeet, followed by Moishele, went to the lower door of the exit compartment. Tuvia was there, waiting for them.

"Open lower door," ordered Ori. Tuvia pressed a button and the door opened. "First ones, into the compartment!" Tuvia reached out and helped the men step in.

"Close lower door!"

Tuvia bade the men good luck and closed the door.

"Open water faucet."

Two openings showed in the wall of the compartment, and a torrent of water rushed in.

"Diving helmets on!" ordered Dani, affixing Azeet's helmet to her head. The water was rising swiftly. Dani and Moishele put flippers on their feet.

Azeet, much smaller than the men, was already under water when they were only hip deep in it. Dani watched her; she was breathing easily and regularly. Delighted, Dani reached down and patted her head. The water was now almost at ceiling height. The men, helmets tight, were below the surface.

"Open upper exit!" ordered Ori through the intercom. Dani reached out and lowered the hatch. The sea water and the water in the compartment

now mixed together, and the three floated up. Azeet paddled alongside Dani. Moishele came up from behind, and soon the heads of the three were above water. Azeet already knew what to do; she raised her right paw and pushed the helmet away from her face to her neck.

"My gosh! This dog is clever!" exclaimed Moishele in wonder. But Dani was already peering about in all directions through his waterproof binoculars, sweeping the horizon from one end to the other. No patrol boat was in sight. "That's good!" he whispered to himself.

Inside the sub, Ori ordered the radio antenna to be set up. Above the water, the tip of the antenna was joined to the periscope. "Dani? Ori here. Can you hear me?"

"This is Dani. I hear you," replied Dani into his transmitter. "Not an enemy craft in sight. You can surface. Over."

"I hear you, Dani. We are surfacing at once. Get away from the sub a bit, away from the whirlpool. Over."

"I hear you. Operation on. End."

Ori turned to the intercom. "We are surfacing," he announced. "Empty tanks one, two, three, in that order."

Nose pointing up, the sub rose to the surface in the deepening darkness. The main hatch was flung open and Dani's four men rushed out with the rubber boat, which they threw into the water. A small outboard motor was attached to its stern. Immediately the men climbed aboard. Each found his oar and the four began rowing quietly.

"Sssss . . . ssss . . ." came the signal from Dani. The four in the rubber boat rowed in the direction of the sound. The heads of the two men and the dog were bobbing in the water. The three were drawn up into the boat. Dani took his seat at the prow, Azeet at his side.

The submarine had disappeared, leaving the men on their own. They kept rowing until Dani, again making sure that no patrol boat was nearby, switched on the outboard motor. The motor purred softly and the boat sped on. Faint wisps of foam glistened in the rays of the rising moon, but Dani felt that speed was as important as caution.

Azeet crouched at the bottom of the boat, her nose up in the air. After all the hours in the helicopter and the sub, she was happy to breathe the fresh sea air. The waves grew higher as the boat neared the port. Every now and then a wave would break over the prow, spraying Azeet's face with salty water. Azeet's tongue told her that this was not drinking water. Her eyes were almost closed against the spray and the wind.

"Slow down," ordered Dani. Through his binoculars he could distinguish the outline of a military jetty. The crucial test was at hand. "Back to the oars," he whispered.

The men cut the motor, and the oars again sliced through the water. Each man knew how to handle his oar, and the boat moved on with hardly a sound. Dani's forehead was wrinkled in worrying. The high waves would make it difficult to climb the jetty, with its steep walls and sharp stones. The waves might even throw the men against the walls and injure them. The rowing slowed down. The boat was close enough for the men to see movement along the jetty. It was bound to be guarded. Moishele remembered that an antiaircraft gun was supposed to be mounted there.

"Good that you've reminded me," Dani said to him. "Let's see if we can locate it."

They saw the gun. Near it were the figures of three men. Dani and Moishele scanned the jetty carefully. Almost directly ahead they saw a sentry, pacing back and forth. Another sentry was on guard a few steps away. The Egyptians were evidently afraid that they would be attacked again and had therefore set up a strong guard.

Azeet kept her eyes on Dani. She sensed that soon she would be called on to do her part, and she waited for an order. Dani pointed to the sentry. Azeet knew that he was a sentry by what he was doing—and she also knew how to attack one when ordered to do so. She saw Dani point to the jetty. The idea of being on firm ground again also tempted her. She raised her left paw and tugged at Dani's suit.

"What's up, Azeet, old girl?" Dani asked. Then he saw her nose pointing at the sentry.

"Say, Dani," whispered Moishele, also aware of what Azeet's nose was doing. "It may be a good idea. If Azeet gets onto the jetty, the sentry won't suspect that she's an Israeli dog. He probably won't touch her."

"You may be perfectly right," Dani whispered back, "but I don't think that it's the thing to do. After all, we brought Azeet along to find Gadi and his men, not to help us get rid of sentries."

"True," admitted Moishele, "but she just might do that very thing."

"Okay," agreed Dani. "It's worth a try. Here's how we'll do it. Azeet will swim over there. We'll dive after her. Two of the men will dive down and swim to the other side of the jetty to find Gadi. Two will remain here in the boat."

Dani repeated the instructions to the others. A few seconds later two of the men dived under and disappeared.

"Go ahead, Azeet," whispered Dani, pointing to the sentry.

Azeet slid into the water quietly and began swimming, keeping her eyes on the sentry. Dani and Moishele also slipped into the water, dropping deep so as to leave no trace. The other two men remained in the boat.

Azeet's movements were almost invisible. Her legs worked quickly but left no trail of foam on the surface. The bubbles which formed at the nape of her neck as her head cut through the water were quickly erased by the waves that came rolling in. The dog was now close enough to the jetty to catch the waves as they rebounded from the wall. She moved closer, smelling the earth close by. Her legs touched the stones of the jetty, but before she could dig in, a huge wave hurled her against the wall. Azeet's legs tried to clamp themselves on to the stones, but the receding water was too strong. For a moment she lost her balance and turned over on her back.

Dani and Moishele, safe from the waves above them, were already at the base of the jetty, waiting for Azeet to make her move. The seconds ticked away quickly. Azeet regained her balance. But now the sentry had halted, as if sensing some kind of movement. He peered all around him nervously but saw nothing but the same waves breaking against the wall. Nothing suspicious could be seen along the jetty itself. "Just a strong wave, probably," he thought and resumed his pacing.

Azeet tried again. Most of her strength was gone, but she had enough left to press forward. She turned her head just in time to see a huge wave rolling toward her. Like an expert swimmer, she let herself be carried by the wave, legs stuck out in front of her like a pair of oars, almost to the top of the jetty. Here the undertow was weak, and Azeet was able to hold on to the stones. A glance upward showed that the top of the jetty was only a short distance away. Azeet began to creep up, slowly. Another wave came up, and this one took her to the very top, almost sweeping her across the jetty into the water on the other side. This time Azeet dug her claws into the stones and held on.

Now her task was to overcome the sentry. She waited until his back was turned and climbed to the top of the jetty. Her feet pattered on the bare stone but the sound was lost in the swishing of the waves. Azeet stepped up her pace. She had three ways in which to jump the sentry—she could hurl herself at him, throw him down and stand over him, or hit him and bowl him over.

Azeet's senses told her that the best way would be to knock him over—and she was right! The sentry was almost at the end of the jetty when Azeet's body hit him like a cannonball. The attack was so sharp that the sentry found himself in the water before he could tell what and who had hit him. His rifle flew in the air and dropped into the water, straight to the bottom. He would not bother us for a while.

Azeet stood where she was, breathing heavily. Dani and Moishele, their heads just above the water at the base of the jetty, grinned at each other joyfully. But there was still work to be done. The gun crew had to be put out of commission before the rubber boat could get beyond the jetty to the port. Dani raised himself out of the water. The second sentry was nowhere in sight; he had either gone off duty or had joined the gun crew. Dani pointed to the other end of the jetty. "Go, Azeet!" he whispered.

Azeet wagged her tail to show that she was glad to see Dani again, then trotted off toward the gun. Dani and Moishele swam along the base of the jetty. Now that the sentry was out of the way, they decided to stay on the surface and keep Azeet in sight. Once she distracted the attention of the crew, they would come up from behind and overpower the guards, without having to use guns and wake up the entire port. Azeet was now near the gun. She could smell people but saw nothing moving. Azeet began to growl, hoping to get something going; otherwise she couldn't know what to do next. She wanted to leap forward, but Dani had only said "Go!"—not "Grab hold!" She went on slowly, growling.

Suddenly one of the gun crew caught sight of her. With a cry of "Devil, devil!" he jumped up on the gun and leveled his rifle at Azeet.

The commander of the crew struck the rifle aside. "What are you trying to do?" he demanded. "Wake up the port? Don't you see that it's just a dog?"

The guard on the gun kept shaking with fright.

"Here, dog, come here," the commander called to Azeet. "Come on," he urged, as Azeet took another step forward, then stopped. Her orders were to go on, but her senses were against it. The Egyptian had a rifle in his hand, and his tone was not too friendly. The Egyptian didn't understand what was holding Azeet back. He rose and came out of the gun position. "Come, good doggie," he urged.

This was the moment for which Dani had been waiting. He made a sign to Moishele to follow him. The two Egyptians by the gun were watching their commander and the dog. Azeet caught sight of Dani and Moishele pulling themselves up to the edge of the jetty. She stepped back in order to draw the Egyptian away. He was still moving toward her when Dani and Moishele leaped at the two guards and clamped their hands on their mouths. The two made no outcry but the commander heard something behind him and turned around. As he did so, Azeet pounced on him and knocked him down flat on the ground. The rifle slipped from his grasp and slid along the jetty—straight to the gun emplacement. Moishele grabbed it with his free hand and pointed it at the Egyptian. "Up with your hands, and come here!" he ordered.

The Egyptian came closer, hands high in the air, with Azeet behind him. Dani had already tied one of the Egyptians to the antiaircraft gun, and Moishele helped him tie up the others. The rule was: Don't kill if you don't have to.

Next, the two threw the gun shells into the water and removed the firing pin. The gun was now useless. So far, everything had gone as planned. Dani reached out and patted Azeet on the head. "Thanks, old girl. With you along, we'll get the job done."

The way to the port was now open for the rubber boat, and the search for Gadi could begin. But as Azeet and her two companions slid back into the water, a series of explosions churned up the water and tossed them around like stalks of straw.

"Depth charges!" whispered Dani. "The Egyptians must be setting them off from time to time, just in case any of our boys are still under water. It's our good luck that the blasts are some distance away. I hope Gadi and the others are out of range."

Moishele handed Dani a small rope. "Better

that we keep in touch this way," he said, "so that the blasts won't separate us." Still swimming they tied the rope to each other and to Azeet.

Dani took his transmitter out of its case and began calling: "Gadi, Gadi. Dani here. Do you hear me?"

No answer. The three kept on swimming, keeping a careful lookout.

A call came through the receiver; it was one of the two other divers: "We've looked among the ships at the pier. Nothing there. We're going on along the beach."

"Good to hear from you," returned Dani. "In that case we'll head there, too! We'll put on our helmets and swim underwater to the beach."

Moishele adjusted Azeet's helmet, and the three went down into the black water. The rope that held them together helped them keep an even pace. More explosions came, but the waves they churned up were weak. Ahead, the buildings of the town loomed up behind the port, but the shoreline was hardly visible. All at once a cliff towered above them.

"That's it," whispered Moishele. "I recall that there should be cliffs and caves in this area."

Dani nodded. Again he called Gadi through the transmitter, and again there was no answer.

"Helmets off," said Dani, taking Azeet's off her nose. Azeet didn't know Gadi, but Dani was hoping that she would come on the scent of people —Gadi and his men, in all likelihood.

A sound of voices came from the top of the cliff.

Moishele knew Arabic. "Those are the coast guards," he said to Dani. "They're looking for somebody."

"Probably Gadi," said Dani. "They couldn't have discovered the tied-up gun crew so soon. Come on. Azeet, search!"

With the dog in the lead, the group went on swimming along the base of the cliff. Every now and then, an inlet of water cut into the cliff, and Dani watched Azeet for some sign that she had found something. Azeet went on swimming, searching for a scent. Suddenly there was a swish in the water. Dani and Moishele stopped short, but Azeet pulled them forward. For some reason she seemed to be happy.

Dani and Moishele didn't want to take any chances. They remained where they were, hugging the dark wall. Suddenly, almost at their feet, two figures came out of the water—the other two divers.

"What the devil!" muttered Dani. "We could have killed you."

"That's right," said the divers. "We almost died laughing at the thought of how we would scare you."

"Good, good," grumbled Moishele. "You're real comedians. Have you found anything to be so happy about?"

The others shook their heads. "No, nothing. We've searched the beach for almost a mile, inch by inch. Not a sign of them."

"We'll do it again, together," Dani decided, "in the same direction. It doesn't make sense that

Gadi should have remained close to the military port. Azeet may yet spot him."

"How about letting her loose on her own?" suggested Moishele.

"Good idea," agreed Dani. He undid the rope which held Azeet to him. "Go, Azeet, go ahead," he whispered, pointing toward the shoreline.

With the four reunited divers swimming easily behind her, Azeet stepped up her pace. The voices on the cliff overhead didn't bother her.

Suddenly the beam of a searchlight flooded the area, cutting through the darkness and playing on the calm waters of the harbor. One of the divers wanted to go under as the beam came sweeping toward them, and Azeet ignored it altogether, but Moishele said, "In such cases it's best to freeze where you are. It's almost impossible to see anything small in this beam, especially when there isn't any motion. That's why it's smart not to move."

From one of the narrow inlets into the caves a new smell came to Azeet's nostrils, something which she hadn't scented elsewhere along the cliffs. It hit her nose like a strong wave. She stopped, and so did the men behind her.

"Ready for encounter," Dani whispered to them. "Go ahead, Azeet."

Azeet wasn't sure. The scent was familiar. It wasn't like the smell of the Egyptians on the jetty. It was something like Dani's, but there was another, unfamiliar smell there, too. The four men watched her but could do nothing. This was something that Azeet would have to figure out herself.

Azeet made up her mind. She swam quickly into the inlet and the cave, Dani and the others behind her. The walls of the cave at that point were almost touching. It was pitch black inside. A slight sound reached their ears.

Dani felt Azeet urging them forward, and he decided to take a chance. "Gadi! Gadi! Are you there?" he called.

"Dani—is that you?" came a voice out of the darkness.

"Right. What happened?"

"We are done in. How did you get in through this narrow entrance? We have a guard posted at the larger one, to your right."

"We have Azeet here, and she pointed the way. Her nose caught your scent. What's the strange smell?"

"Don't ask. All of us are wounded. As soon as we finished our operation and looked for a hiding place, the Egyptians filled the harbor with depth charges. The waves they caused threw us against the cliff. We're a bunch of broken bones. Did you bring a rubber boat? Josh and Asher can't move, and the rest of us aren't too much better off."

"Don't worry," Dani called into the darkness. "We have a boat. Two of us will go out to bring it here. We'll tell them to stand by."

Moishele went back to the entrance. From a distance came the blast of depth charges. The searchlight beam was now directed at the sky.

Were they looking for planes? Moishele wondered. He took out his transmitter.

"Boat? Moishele here. Over."

"Moishele! Good to hear you. We're at the same spot where you left us. Can you flash a signal to us? Over."

"Wait. End." Moishele swam back into the cave and reported to Dani.

A flash signal seemed to Dani to be too risky. Somebody would have to swim out and bring the boat in. But how could he find the cave again?

"I'll do it, Dani," whispered Moishele, "if you let me have Azeet. Together we'll turn the trick perfectly."

"Okay. Take your transmitter."

"Come on, Azeet," said Moishele.

"Go with him, Azeet," added Dani.

"See you soon," said Moishele, as he and Azeet left the cave and headed out into the harbor, toward the open sea. Moishele took his bearings and tried to locate the jetty through his binoculars. But Azeet didn't wait. Her senses led her in exactly the right direction, and she swam sturdily ahead on a beeline. Moishele knew that her "radar" was reliable, and he kept right behind her.

The two reached the jetty in a matter of minutes. Moishele checked to see if any coast guard boats were in the area, but nothing appeared to be moving on the water. Moishele shook his head; the absence of the coast guard was good for the safety of the rubber boat, but a single boat moving in the harbor might easily be spotted.

Azeet swam directly to the end of the jetty. No sound came from above. The gun crew was probably still tied and gagged.

"Ssss, sss," came the familiar hiss from among the rocks of the breakwater.

"Ssss, sss," replied Moishele. By this time Azeet was already near the boat.

There was no time for an exchange of greetings. Moishele climbed aboard and joined the other two at the oars. Azeet turned around, ready to lead.

"Go ahead, Azeet!"

The dog was really excited. She streaked ahead, and the three men, working their oars frantically in the six-man boat, had a hard time keeping up with her.

"It's good we have Azeet with us," grunted Moishele, breathing heavily. Every minute seemed to drag on for hours. "By myself I might have found the cave—in a couple of years."

Azeet kept on. The shoreline drew nearer and nearer. Again the houses atop the cliff loomed in the darkness, and the sound of waves lapping against the cliff grew stronger. Almost before Moishele could judge the remaining distance the boat was at the cave entrance.

Dani was there, waiting. "All hail Azeet, chief navigator," he said softly, patting Azeet on the head.

The men inside the cave began to come out.

The wounded were helped into the rubber boat by the others. Suddenly the searchlight beam came sweeping toward the spot, stopping a few yards away.

"Don't move," warned Dani. "Stay where you are." They all froze in position.

The beam moved again, sweeping closer to the boat. From the top of the cliff came excited voices. Had the Egyptian sentries spotted the boat? Dani waited for the beam to move away, then, in a split second, drew the boat back into the entrance to the cave, out of sight from above.

The wounded in the boat were shivering from the cold and the tension. Another night in the open—and perhaps capture . . .

The beam returned and remained steady on the cliff.

"They must have gotten on to something," Dani whispered to Gadi. "We must get out of here right away. See that the wounded are all in the boat and start the motor as you head out to the open sea, at full speed. We'll swim underwater and keep in touch with you by transmitter or flash. The sub is waiting with its antenna up. Let's go."

Gadi checked to see that all the wounded were aboard and slid into the prow seat. The others grabbed the oars and waited.

"Go ahead," Dani said, giving the boat a shove out of the cave. The oars dipped noiselessly into the water, but the men, their muscles stiff from the cold, were hardly able to keep the boat going.

Only slowly the boat moved forward, with Dani, Moishele and Azeet swimming ahead of it.

Without warning, the flashing beam fastened itself on the group. From the cliff a hail of bullets covered the area.

"Switch on the motor," cried Gadi.

"Dive!" echoed Dani, leading the way down to make room for the boat.

The motor spurted into life and the boat immediately picked up speed. Gadi put it in a zigzag course and was able to outdistance the bullets, even though the beam still followed them.

Dani adjusted Azeet's helmet and the group continued under water. Dani gritted his teeth; again it was Gadi's luck to be in the thick of the fire. And there was still the narrow opening of the breakwater. "It's good that we put the gun crew out of business," he thought. "One burst from that cannon would blow the boat apart."

The shooting stopped, but from the port came the sound of motors. The Egyptians were sending their patrol boats out. Fortunately, the breakwater interfered with the searchlight, and the rubber boat passed by into the open sea. But only a short distance behind came two patrol boats, their smaller searchlights playing about around on the water. The swimmers swam with their heads out so they could move faster.

Suddenly a blast came from the direction of the patrol boats. Streaks of fire showed on their decks. Their guns and searchlights were trained upward.

Before Dani could figure all this out, a voice came through his instrument.

"Dani, this is Ori. We thought it best to make our presence felt in the neighborhood, just in case. Keep going according to plan. Over."

Dani couldn't believe his ears. "Ori, this is Dani. Your presence has set two little old Egyptian boats on fire. We're on our way. Over."

The patrol boats were now streaking back to the port, as the wind fanned the flames on their decks.

By the time Azeet reached the submarine, the sleek craft had already surfaced and was waiting to take the men aboard. One after another, the crew hauled them up onto the sub's deck. Ori was on hand to welcome them aboard.

The Egyptian coastal batteries now went into action. Shells struck the water close to the sub and the men were sprayed thoroughly.

"All accounted for," reported Dani.

Ori rushed back to the control room. "Ready to submerge. All hatches down. Fill tanks. Depth one hundred feet. Azimuth sixty degrees. Full speed ahead. Head for home."

Dani stripped the diving gear off Azeet's back, as one of the crewmen set a bowl of milk before her.

Azeet lapped up a bit of the milk, then had the treat she liked most—to be scratched on her back by Dr. Harubi.

4. TANK BATTLE IN THE DESERT

Do you remember the story of King Solomon and the Queen of Sheba? The Queen ruled over the Land of Ophir, which once flourished far to the south of the Red Sea, at the tip of the Arabian Peninsula.

This far-away land can be reached by overland routes in many days' travel in a scorching desert of blazing sands and over winding trails across snow-capped mountains. It is a difficult and tiring journey. It can also be reached by sea. A sailboat leaving Eilat with a north wind behind it can skim across a long tongue of water the length of the Sinai Peninsula, to the Red Sea. But at the end of this tongue—the Bay of Akaba—the waterway becomes a very narrow passage, closed in by the Sinai Peninsula on the west and the island of Tiran on the east, which extend their underwater coral reefs far into the water, leaving but a scant safe strip for boats to pass through. These are the Straits of Solomon, known today as the Straits of Tiran, originally named for the king who sent many ships through the straits on their way to trade with distant lands.

All straits, or water passages, of this kind are open to the ships of all nations. Only pirates dared attack merchant ships in these waterways, and they quickly made off with their loot, leaving the straits open. Nations of the world make treaties among themselves, recognizing the right of all ships to passage through all the straits.

For Israelis, passage through the Straits of Solomon is more important today than in ancient times. We have built a large city at Eilat, and our trade with foreign lands, such as Iran and Japan, is growing all the time. We import raw materials, and we send them farm produce and industrial items.

The Egyptians are well aware of the importance of the straits to Israel. One bright day in May 1967, they closed the straits to Israeli ships. Moreover, they stepped up the activity of their raiders and, together with other Arab countries, organized a large joint army which they claimed would make war on Israel.

Israel countered with major military action of its own. The long desert routes were quickly jammed with fleeing Egyptian troops pursued by the Israel Defence Forces. Israeli armored vehicles carved new trails out of the desert sands, catching the Egyptians unaware.

Dr. Harubi was in military service with one of the tank units. His ambulance sped after the swift tanks—and Azeet sat at his side. In no time at all the ambulance was covered with the fine desert dust churned up by the tank treads. Dr. Harubi's hair and Azeet's fur changed color and became the brownish yellow of the desert.

The tanks advanced so swiftly in pursuit of the enemy that the fuel trucks couldn't keep up with them on the difficult roads. The Air Corps had to come in and drop down containers of water and fuel to enable the tanks to keep going.

In one of the battles Nir, the commander of one of the tanks, caught sight of an Egyptian convoy trying to get away by a side route. Nir gave orders to Gili, the driver, over the intercom: "Driver, half left, go ahead."

Adi, the gunner, heard the command and began turning the tank turret toward the enemy. Despite the heavy fire all around him, Nir remained on his feet, the upper part of his body protruding from the turret in order to keep watch on the Egyptian column. Adi and Gili also spotted the target. Hami, the commander of the tank unit, didn't notice that Nir's tank had turned, and Nir was so intent on pursuit that he simply forgot to let Hami know what he was doing. Nir wanted to overtake the Egyptian convoy and stop it, but the road was so narrow that it was impossible to outflank the convoy.

Adi's accurate firing kept hitting the convoy. Tanks and trucks were caught and had to be abandoned alongside the road. Nir, watching from the turret, urged Gili to go faster. Now Nir tried to get in touch with Hami and tell him what was happening, but the hills interfered with the radio and the message didn't get through. Nir decided to go on alone. But he wasn't quite alone. Behind him came bouncing Dr. Harubi's ambulance. The clouds of dust churned up in the tank battle had caused the doctor to lose the main body of the unit and follow Nir's tank instead. True, he wondered why there weren't more tanks ahead of him, but not for a moment did he hesitate. He had learned long ago that the men of the Israeli army knew what they were doing.

So Dr. Harubi sat behind the wheel of the ambulance and drove past the burning Egyptian vehicles, with his Uzi gun on his knees and Azeet on the seat beside him. The whine of bullets fired by the retreating Egyptians caused both to crouch low. The doctor drove with his eyes just above the rim of the wheel.

Nir was in high spirits. He really had put quite a few Egyptian tanks out of business. He kept going, unaware that it was almost sunset. Gili, however, was checking the instrument panel. When he looked at the fuel gauge, he became frightened; the needle was almost at zero!

"Nir," he called, "we're just about out of gas!"

Nir didn't take his eyes off the Egyptian tanks. "Don't worry," he replied. "We'll take care of these few tanks and go back."

Adi had been firing without letup. Now, glancing at his stock of shells, he saw that there were only seven left.

"Nir," he said. "I've got only seven more shells."

"Fine," said Nir. "That should take care of seven tanks. Besides, it's getting dark, and you won't be able to do much with your cannon."

Dr. Harubi looked at his watch. The growing darkness worried him. The prospect of spending the night in the desert wasn't very appealing; besides, Hami and the unit might need the ambulance.

Suddenly there was a loud explosion. The ambulance tilted to one side. Dr. Harubi felt something strike him in the head. Just before he blacked out he saw that the explosion had torn the tank tread. The tank stopped in its tracks. Nir jumped down from the turret to see what was the matter. The Egyptians, feeling more secure at night, had stopped and opened fire. A bullet hit Nir in the shoulder, and he went down.

Adi swiveled the turret toward the oncoming Egyptians and stopped them with a well-aimed shell. Gili jumped off the tank and ran to Nir's side, loosening his first-aid kit as he ran. He quickly bandaged Nir's wound. The Egyptian fire grew heavier. Adi switched from the cannon to the machine gun and kept up a steady stream of fire at the enemy. Now only one Egyptian was left —a sharpshooter hidden in a nearby gully. But his fire was enough to keep the tank and the ambulance pinned down.

Dr. Harubi came to. His head ached terribly. He raised it, then dropped back—fortunately— for in that split second the sharpshooter sent a bullet right through the open window of the ambulance.

The doctor caught sight of Azeet, crouching tensely on her haunches. "Grab him, Azeet," he whispered. "Go get him!"

Azeet set her tail wagging. She sensed that she wasn't to show herself in the open window. She crept up to it and waited.

The rattle of machine gun fire outside mingled with the ping of the sniper's rifle. Azeet felt that this was her moment to move. She streaked out through the window and flattened herself on the sand—just as the sniper turned his rifle on her.

Gili, safe with Nir behind the disabled tank, saw Azeet leave the ambulance. He reached into the tank seat for his intercom and made contact with Adi, perched behind the machine gun. "Keep the Egyptian busy," he called. "I think that Azeet is going to do something."

"Okay," Adi replied briefly. He, too, had been hit in the arm, but the wound wasn't deep.

Gili went over to Nir. "We have to keep holding the sniper's attention," he said. "I'll try it with my Uzi. Keep down."

Nir didn't like the idea of being out of action. He turned over on his side, grasped his own Uzi, and began crawling to the other end of the tank.

Dr. Harubi opened the ambulance door a crack and saw Azeet on the sand, waiting. "Grab him, Azeet, grab him!" he called again.

Without waiting another second, Azeet dashed across the open space to the gully, unobserved in the darkness. As Adi and Gili went on firing, she crept along the bottom of the gully, careful not to make the slightest sound.

Gili ran out of ammunition. There were more clips in the tank, but to climb aboard the tank was much too risky. He went over to Nir and kept firing with his Uzi.

Azeet was now so close to the Egyptian that she could smell him. She was also so close that Adi and Gili were afraid that they might shoot her as they fired on the sniper. In the meantime, the dog worked her way to the rear of the Egyptian, so that she would not be caught in line with his rifle. He was on his knees, peering over the edge of the gully. This was a bad situation for Azeet. What good would it do to attack the sniper's feet? As it was, there was hardly any room in the gully to move around.

Dr. Harubi was following Azeet's course in his mind, and he knew at once what his dog was up against. If he could get the Egyptian to turn around and see Azeet he would be scared out of his wits. Dr. Harubi decided to put his knowledge of Arabic to good, if daring, use. He called to Adi and Gili to stop firing, then shouted,

"Hey, Egyptian! The devil's behind you!" To Azeet he shouted, in Hebrew, "Grab hold of his foot!"

Azeet gave the Egyptian's trousers a hefty yank. The Egyptian turned around. At the sight of Azeet's bared fangs he forgot everything else. With one leap he was out of the gully. Adi and Gili held their fire. They were afraid of hitting Azeet. Besides, it was unfair to shoot the Egyptian when he was practically defenseless.

Azeet did the rest. It took one bound for her to

catch up with the fleeing Egyptian and clamp her jaw around his shooting arm. The rifle dropped to the sand. The Egyptian fought wildly to shake her off, but Azeet, letting go of his arm, halted him in his tracks by doing a little dance to bar his way. Finally tiring of this maneuver, Azeet leaped at the cowed Egyptian and knocked him down. When Gili came running, he found Azeet astride her captive, very much pleased with herself. She slipped off to let the Egyptian get up.

Nir decided to let the sniper go. There was no sense in holding him captive when they themselves were cut off in the desert.

"*Yalla*, get going, away from here," Gili told the Egyptian. The man was a soldier and deserved a break.

The Egyptian couldn't believe his ears, but he lost no time moving off. "Many thanks, sir," he said. "Allah shall repay you."

"Good, good, get going," Gili called after the Egyptian's vanishing figure. He motioned to Azeet, who was squatting on the Egyptian's rifle, and the two went back to the ambulance.

Dr. Harubi was waiting for them. His head was throbbing like a pump, but he went over to Nir and examined him. "He's got to have a lot of water," he said to Gili and Adi as he adjusted Nir's bandage.

The two went over to the side of the tank where the water cans were fastened, only to find that Egyptian bullets had punctured every single can, and there wasn't a drop of water left.

"There's water in the ambulance," Dr. Harubi said.

But here, too, the water can had fallen victim to the shooting. Even the radiator was full of holes. The only water left was what the men had in their canteens.

"No reason to worry," Dr. Harubi cheered the others. "The water in the canteen can last a long time. Besides, if a rescue unit doesn't reach us, we'll send Azeet to find a water hole."

"Okay," decided Nir. "Let's eat something. Besides, some water may be left on those Egyptian vehicles we knocked out."

Adi went to look for some dry undergrowth, while Gili opened cans of meat and sardines and passed around some halvah for a quick energy pickup. Dr. Harubi took a can of meat out of the ambulance for Azeet. Nir took the undergrowth which Adi had found and lighted a fire for tea. They didn't post a sentry. They didn't have to— not with Azeet on hand.

Suddenly, lights showed in the distance. Adi ran to the tank and opened the communications instrument. Hami's voice came through:

"Nir! Hami here. Do you hear me? Over."

"Hami, this is Adi. Hear you like a bell. We can also see your lights. Over."

"This is Hami. We're coming. What happened to you? Over."

"Adi here. We went up on a mine. Nir has a slight shoulder wound. Over."

"Hami here. We'll be there right away. End."

Half an hour later the tank unit was there. Hami jumped down from the turret and headed straight for Nir. "What did you do? What's this business? That's not nice."

Nir shrugged his shoulders and grimaced with pain. "Well, it happens. What's new with you?"

"Fine. In fact, I hate to admit it but you fellows did us a good turn. By going after the Egyptian column you broke up their plan for regrouping and you gained control of this road. We'll use it in the morning for a flanking attack."

As he was talking, the tank-unit mechanics were already busily repairing the tread of Nir's damaged tank.

Nir told Hami how Azeet had handled the situation.

Hami looked at the dog. "Fine," he decided. "We'll recommend her for a merit citation."

As soon as the repairs were done, Nir's tank was filled with fuel and ammunition. Nir insisted on taking his place in the turret. The others helped him up into it.

"Dr. Harubi and Azeet will ride with me until morning," decided Nir. The ambulance was hardly worth towing. "Dr. Harubi will help Adi load the cannon, if necessary, and Azeet will be chief lookout."

Gili got the motor going. Hami went back to the lead tank, and a moment later the command came through the communications of all the tanks: "Tanks ahead." Gili swunk his tank into the column. Azeet, sitting next to him, stuck her head out. The desert sand was swirling from under the tank, a shimmering curtain of gold in the headlights. The cool night desert air swept across Azeet's nostrils. She let her tongue hang out and breathed deeply. Gili grinned at her.

Nir picked up the microphone. "Hami, this is Azeet's tank. Everything's fine. Going ahead with you. End."

5. IN THE HILLS OF MOAB

Long and narrow, the valley of the Jordan stretches for many miles, from the Sea of Galilee in the north to the Dead Sea in the south. On both sides the valley is flanked by tall mountain ranges: to the west lie the mountains of Judea and Samaria, while to the east are the mountains of Moab and Bashan. Down through this valley runs a deep ravine—the course of the Jordan River. Its waters bring life to the soil near the riverbed, and its banks are lined with thorny reeds and needlelike pines.

In the winter, the Jordan rises and overflows its banks, turning the ravine into a spongy, swamplike jungle. Even in the summer, when the water runs low in the riverbed, there are still many spots where one can easily sink, or drown, and at these points no one dares to ford the river. But there are also safe and shallow fords where the river can be crossed on a raft or by holding on to a rope stretched taut across the water.

Every now and then Jordanian troops and

bands of marauders try to cross the Jordan into Israel, to strike at army bases and at the new settlements along the valley. But Israeli units have learned how they operate and have come up with ways of handling them.

The paratroopers stationed in the valley, Azeet's faithful fans, lost no time getting her to help them. Overnight she became known as "queen of the valley." Covering many miles each day, Azeet would streak along the patrol roads and the side trails, sniffing at the ground for the familiar scent of the marauders. Their clothes and weapons, the food they carried, and especially their mud-covered boots would cause Azeet's sensitive nostrils to twitch and lead her to the enemy as if with a magnet. Once she had tracked down something suspicious, she would stick to the scent and would not give up until she had located the marauders and had led the paratroopers to their hiding places.

The mountain ranges that rise westward from the valley floor are very difficult for tracking. Hardly anything grows on their slopes, since the soil is hard and barren. A foot stepping there leaves only a faint scent, and even this is likely to evaporate quickly in the wind and fade in the powerful rays of the blazing sun.

In the blistering, throat-parching days of summer, Azeet's grim perseverance was more than a match for the will and endurance of the marauders. While they usually took it easy in the cool of the caves in the area, Azeet would leap to her task, dry tongue hanging out and her breath coming in quick pants, until she would come to a halt near the very mouth of the cave where the enemy was hiding, as if to say, "They're in here!"

Azeet's reputation soon reached the ears of all the marauders. From their hiding places they kept a sharp lookout for her. They knew that if she was anywhere around, their position would soon be discovered, and capture would follow soon enough. In most cases they did nothing; they simply hoped that the dog wouldn't find them. At times, enraged and despairing, they would take a pot shot at her, from a distance. Luckily they always missed—and one shot was enough to send Azeet to cover. Usually her instincts told her to stay beyond the reach of the bullets. The marauders liked to think that she had been hit, or had lost the scent, but soon enough, somewhere near the cave or above it, Azeet would show herself—with the Israeli unit not far behind.

Later, the Israelis began hitting the marauders in their own territory, on the other side of the Jordan. Here, too, Azeet led the way. Her unerring senses led the men straight to the houses where the marauders were hiding. Watching her closely, the soldiers were also able to decide on what kind of action they should take.

Azeet became a good-luck charm. Every unit wanted her along on its operations. One day, Moishele was summoned by his commanding officer and given a tough assignment.

"You are to take a unit and strike at a

marauder command base, deep in enemy territory. We've figured out that you need a whole night to carry out the operation. This means that you won't be able to allow even one hour for mistakes or some unforeseen event. You will have to know every inch of your advance route and your return route, because you won't have time to go looking for a road. You are also to try to take the enemy by surprise, to keep your own men from getting hurt. Just in case you do get into trouble, we'll have helicopters and rescue units standing by from the moment that you cross the Jordan. At the enemy base there are secret documents about the marauders' plans and operations. It's very important that you bring these back with you."

The officer opened a drawer, took out a rolled-up bundle, and handed it to Moishele. "Here you'll find the maps and the aerial photos that you'll need, plus further orders. The staff officers will supply you with all the equipment and information. Any questions?"

"No, sir. Thank you. Everything's clear." Moishele saluted and turned to leave. At the door, with his hand already on the knob, he hesitated and looked back. "Can I take Azeet with me—I hope?"

The officer grinned. "I was waiting for that. Sure you can."

"Thanks a lot." Moishele grinned back and went out.

By evening the unit was all set to move. From the nearby field a clattering noise announced the arrival of the helicopters, ready for action. The rescue unit was waiting in the command car, its headlights pointing two bright fingers into the gathering darkness.

Moishele made a final inspection of his men's gear, to make sure that nothing was missing. Each man jumped up and down, in turn, to make sure that his gear did not rattle. Shirt sleeves were rolled down and all buttons fastened as protection against mosquito bites and the thorny undergrowth.

The medic came up with a bottle of anti-insect lotion and passed it around. "Smear it all over the exposed skin surface, fellows, face included," he said. "Be careful not to get it into your eyes. The stuff burns."

Now the men were ready. The commanding officer arrived and the men crowded around him. They all knew him well, and he knew each of them by name. They were all in good spirits. Everyone fell silent, and all eyes were on the commanding officer, as he said, "Men, I don't have to tell you how tough is the task that you are about to carry out. You know it only too well. Very few among the paratroopers have drawn such a dangerous assignment. It's all yours. Good luck. See you in the morning."

He walked along the line of his men, shaking each one's hand. Azeet was squatting at the end of the line. The officer extended his hand. Azeet lifted her right paw and stretched it out toward him. The commander patted her on the head with his other hand, and Azeet stuck out her tongue and licked it warmly.

"Into the car," ordered Moishele. He took his seat next to the driver, Azeet at his feet. The vehicle was soon lost to sight in the darkness, and the unit was on its own. Some distance from the Jordan, the men got out and silently arranged themselves in a single file. Azeet, keeping close to Moishele, went with him to the head of the column.

At first, the going was easy. The men had to cross a few gullies, but, other than the white dust that covered that part of the valley, nothing slowed them down.

It was a different story when they reached the jungle near the riverbank. The spot which Moishele had picked for the crossing was in the very thick of the undergrowth. No Jordanians, he felt sure, would be lying in wait here. No one would even dream that an armed force would dare cross at such a difficult point.

The pace slowed. Moishele and one of the men, Tal, took out their machetes. With long, powerful strokes they hacked away at the dense reeds and the wild raspberry vines, clearing the way for the others. This was a lot of work and took precious time. Azeet, keeping her body low, wriggled through the growth ahead of the men. Every few steps she waited for them to catch up. No enemy was going to surprise them.

The ground grew spongy underfoot, and the men's shoes squeaked in the water. Clouds of mosquitoes and other insects hovered overhead, buzzing angrily because the lotion on the men's skin kept them away. Moishele kept hacking away like a machine, without a moment's rest. The air grew heavy. From the column came muffled curses as the men's weapons and the gear on their backs caught on the tangled growth and jerked them backward. Finally, breathing hard, faces scratched and lashed by the reeds and the vines, the men reached the riverbank. Down below, the water was flowing calmly, and a light breeze came blowing down the ravine.

Azeet glanced at Moishele and waited for the signal to go down into the water. Moishele breathed easier now. So far, so good; if Azeet was all set to go in, it was a sign that no enemy force was around. He loosened a buckle in his belt. Around it a thin, strong cord of nylon was wrapped many times over. Moishele fastened the buckle to the dog's collar and wrapped the end of the cord around his own wrist. He motioned to the men, and they spread out along the bank, guns ready. One of them, Ori, lowered from his back the coil of rope he had been carrying, climbed up a sturdy tree growing by the bank, and tied the rope around a heavy limb and again around the truck. Moishele waited until Ori was done, then patted Azeet on the head and whispered, "Go ahead, girl!"

As the nylon cord unreeled behind her, Azeet slid down the steep bank into the water. Her movements hardly caused a ripple. Moishele kept

his field glasses trained on her in the feeble light, to catch any sign that would tell him that she had spotted something. At the bottom of the slope, after she was already in the water, Azeet paused. Her instinct told her that if the enemy was lurking near by she would have to be doubly careful while crossing. The light breeze brought no suspicious scent to her nostrils. Her paws came out on the muddy bottom, and she began to swim. Despite its outer calm, the current was strong enough to pull Azeet toward the south. Straining against it, with only her head showing above the water, Azeet thrust her body on toward the east bank.

The men held their breath, waiting to see Azeet reach the other side. Moishele's field glasses kept sweeping the other bank, on the lookout for a surprise attack. At last Azeet felt earth beneath her feet. She left the water and shook herself briskly, as dogs do, then began scrambling up the bank. As soon as she got to the top, she went up to a tree and sniffed all around it. She had been trained to tell whether the tree and its roots were strong and sound. She circled the tree, keeping her nose low. Moishele's glasses followed her movements, for this was the crucial moment. Azeet's circling the tree meant that the tree was sturdy enough. She went around it ten times, winding the nylon cord around its trunk. This done, she turned toward the group on the other side of the river and waited.

It was now Ori's move. At a signal from

Moishele, he made one end of the thick rope secure around his waist, took the nylon cord from his commander and, drawing it in as he went, quickly forded the river. On the other side, he paused long enough to pat Azeet on the head, then undid the rope around his waist and tied it to the trunk. Moishele felt his tug at the rope; this was the signal to draw the rope taut and thus form a "bridge" across the ravine. One by one, the men went above the water, each in his own fashion—one like a chameleon, back toward the water below, another one hand over hand, the third crawling astride the rope. In a few minutes all were lined up on the east bank, ready to push on. Ori loosened the rope and let it slide down into the water, where it would remain, unseen in the darkness, until the men were ready to use it again on their way back.

"Psst," hissed Moishele, and the men, once again in a single file, moved on through the thick growth, following Azeet's wriggling body.

Now the jungle was behind them. The men breathed more easily. After all that pushing through the tangled undergrowth, the march in the white dust almost seemed like running. Straight ahead lay the Jordanian positions, protected by ambush points strung out the whole length of the valley. Every once in a while Moishele halted the column and scanned the area through his field glasses. He could make out the positions, but there was no sign of life around. "They don't seem to be expecting us," thought

Moishele, and he led his men to a beaten trail. They could move much faster on it.

One, two, three hours went by. The trail, turning and twisting through the barren hills, seemed endless. At every turn the men thought, "Ah, here's where we see the target"—and each time they were disappointed. Moishele felt himself growing more and more tense. The marauder base, he knew, was on the far side of a hill. If he couldn't locate this particular hill, he might, in error, just about roll down its other side, into the base. Judging by the distance his unit had covered, it had to be very close by.

As he was figuring out his unit's position, comparing the turns in the trail to the map drawing, he saw Azeet returning from her lead position. He patted the dog's head and was about to move on when he found Azeet firmly barring his way.

"That's it," said Moishele to himself. "That's Azeet's way of letting us know we're there."

The men crouched low—as did Azeet—and crept behind her to the top of the hill. They marveled at the way that the dog kept her body low so that it could not be seen against the moonlit skyline.

The twelve men in the unit were to work in groups of four each. Each group had a leader. The three leaders now followed Azeet to the crest of the hill and peered over the edge. There, on the slope, was the marauders' base—three buildings ablaze with lights, although the yard and the spaces between the buildings were dark. The marauders were clearly not expecting the Israelis to stage a raid so deep in Jordanian territory.

Moishele's eyes were glued to the field glasses. He went over the plan of action. As soon as the men were inside the fence they would break up into their groups. Each group would attack a building, break in, gather up all the documents, and blow up the building itself. All the men would then return to the break in the fence and make a swift getaway from the area.

Azeet had done her share and still had to lead the men back along the return route, but she wouldn't remain behind. It was decided to let her go with Moishele's group. All the men were now motioned to come up to the crest. They broke up into the three groups. Moishele took a final look through his glasses. A few sentries were strolling along the fence; otherwise the base seemed to be deserted.

Moishele waited until the sentries had moved away from the spot at the fence which he had picked for the breakthrough, then began to wriggle downward, followed by Azeet and the rest of the force. The barbed wire fell away noiselessly under Moishele's powerful snips. The opening was wide enough and high enough for a quick getaway. Then Moishele had an idea— Azeet could remain at that spot and, by barking, guide the men to it right after the blasts. She could even take care of the sentries, a task for which none of the men could be spared.

"Sit here, Azeet," whispered Moishele. Azeet

didn't quite understand why she was being asked to sit, but she did, and her eyes followed the disappearing figures of the men.

The units separated, each moving cautiously in the shadows toward the objective. Suddenly there was the sound of shooting. One of the sentries had spied the raiders and opened fire. The other sentries immediately rushed to his side to see what was the matter.

"Fire! Follow me!" Moishele shouted. Before his words died away, the air was filled with the familiar sound of bursts from the Uzi guns and exploding grenades. The sentries were cut down.

"To the houses!" came the command. The men moved in rapidly, firing as they ran.

A moment later it was all over. The marauders in the buildings had been put out of action. The raiders quickly emptied the desk drawers and planted the explosives. Moishele raced from house to house to make sure that things were going as planned.

Then Azeet heard a noise, somewhere to her right. Other marauders, hearing the shots, had come up the hill. One look was enough to tell them what was happening, but instead of charging down the hill, they decided to set up an ambush and trap the Israelis on their way back. But they hadn't seen Azeet. The dog immediately understood what the marauders were planning to do. She shot up the slope like a cannonball, made a sharp circle in order to come up behind the marauders, and leaped at them, attacking like a whole pack of wolves. With panic-stricken yells, they dropped their guns and scattered in all directions.

"Set off the charges!" shouted Moishele as Azeet's barking came to his ears.

The three buildings whooshed into the air, all at once. The sight of the flying stones made the fleeing marauders run even faster.

"Back to the opening!" ordered Moishele. "I'll stay behind until you get through. Azeet's barking will guide you."

Fortunately for the men, Azeet had managed to get back to her post in time, and they came running to the hole in the fence. But by this time some of the marauders were back, too, and the sound of the barking gave their location away. Soon bullets were whining above the heads of the men below.

"Quiet now, Azeet," whispered Moishele, as he came running to the fence. Azeet immediately fell silent.

"Everybody accounted for?"

"Everybody."

"Good. Follow me—fast!"

Moving quietly, the men skirted the hill and headed for the open field. Behind them the marauders' fire was dying down.

"We'll have to cut across the fields," said Moishele to himself. "They'll be on the lookout for us along all the roads to the river."

When the men were some distance away from the wrecked base, Moishele had them slow down to a rapid walk. "Head for home, Azeet," he ordered. The dog trotted up to the head of the column and began to lead.

The return journey was like a nightmare. Off the beaten track, the ground was studded with sharp stones. The men moved along half bent over, to keep from showing themselves too much above the ground.

The men were panting. Moishele glanced at his watch. "No time for a rest," he grunted. "If anything should hold us up, we'd either lose a whole day or have to take a chance and call in the helicopter."

Without warning, shots were being fired at the Israelis, from all sides. A Jordanian patrol must have spotted them, called for reinforcements, and set up an ambush. Moishele was hit at once in the stomach.

"Itzik," he called to one of the men. "Take command and keep going. I'll stay behind and cover you. The marauders will think that they have all of us pinned down. When you're a safe distance away, call in the helicopter."

"We won't leave you alone," protested Itzik.

"You have your orders, Itzik," said Moishele sternly. "This is how it has to be. The documents must get to the base at all costs. I'll see you back there. Leave me a light machine gun and grenades." Without another word, he turned on his side, leveled the machine gun, and began firing in the direction of the ambush. Itzik and the others slipped away into the darkness.

No one remembered Azeet in all the excitement, but the dog didn't forget the man who had chosen to stay behind. She crouched behind a large rock a few paces away and kept her eyes on Moishele as he moved from boulder to boulder, dragging himself painfully, firing and throwing grenades. The marauders, thinking that they had trapped the entire unit, now stopped firing. They planned to wait until dawn and then pick off the raiders one by one.

Despite his wound, Moishele smiled to himself. By this time the men and the documents were far away, perhaps even aloft in the helicopter, heading west. Now he could afford to surrender. He called out in Arabic, "Hold your fire! I am alone here, and wounded."

Alone? He didn't know that Azeet was nearby.

The marauders didn't believe what they had heard. "If you are alone," one of them called back, "get up and walk toward us. Keep your hands up!"

Gritting his teeth to hold back the pain, Moishele drew himself to his feet and raised his hands. There was blood all over his clothes. He half stumbled forward in the darkness until a flashlight caught him in its ray. Some of the marauders raised their guns, ready to shoot, but their commander held them back. "Don't shoot him. Not yet. We shall question him first."

Moishele was reeling. As he came toward the Jordanian commander, one of the marauders aimed the butt of his gun at Moishele's head.

Suddenly he gave a yell of pain and dropped his rifle. On his bleeding wrist were the marks of a dog's fangs. Azeet was off into the darkness before the Jordanians knew what was happening. And Moishele was careful not to show them that he knew.

After brief questioning, during which Moishele refused to talk, he was put aboard a jeep and sent with a convoy to the Jordanians' base. He kept thinking about the men—and about Azeet. He didn't know that she was only some fifty yards behind the jeep, loping along in the rays of its tail-lights. Fortunately for her and for Moishele's wound, the jeep wasn't traveling very fast.

The convoy didn't spend much time at the base, and no one bothered to dress Moishele's wound. He was given water but refused it; even a drink of water can be dangerous if you have a hole in your stomach.

The Jordanians could see that Moishele's wound would make it impossible for him to escape. They left him alone in the jeep and went inside the building. Azeet lost no time. A quick leap landed her in the driver's seat. She began licking Moishele's face furiously, just to let him know that she was there.

With a start, Moishele came to his senses. He was relieved to know that the faithful dog was safe and nearby. "You here, Azeet?" He tried to pat her, but his hand dropped weakly to his side.

Voices came through the open windows of the building. Moishele caught the words "prison" and the name of the town Es Salt. He braced himself, found his pen and a piece of paper inside his shirt, and wrote with a trembling hand, "They are taking me to the prison in Es Salt." He crumpled the note, thrust it under the buckle of Azeet's collar, and whispered, "Home, Azeet! Get home! Give them the note! Go!"

The effort was too much for Moishele. His head began to whirl and he slid down in his seat. Azeet kept licking his face and hands, unwilling to leave him despite her orders.

The marauders came out of their headquarters. Azeet vaulted out of the jeep and took cover in the darkness. When the jeep drove away, she streaked off on her mission, but one of the marauders in the yard saw her. Immediately word was flashed from headquarters to all Jordanian positions. The officer in charge guessed right away that this dog was the famous Azeet. And now she was trapped on Jordanian soil! The message was to look out for her and either take her alive or shoot to kill.

Unaware of this danger, Azeet ran forward, her senses fixed on two things—to find the way back and to find water. Her entire body was trembling with thirst, but her inner sense told her that Moishele's life depended on the note tucked under her collar. She sniffed the air until she got her direction—westward. She lengthened her stride, changing her course only to avoid a high hill or falling into a gully. Skirting these obstacles, she stuck to her course.

The night was rapidly drawing to a close, and Azeet was still in the hills of Moab. She knew that she had to find water before daybreak, when she could be seen as she searched for a water hole. She also knew from experience that water was to be found in gullies more readily than on the ridges. She skidded down the side of a deep gully that ran westward and kept going along the bottom.

Soon she scented not only water, but also smoke, people, and animals. Azeet stopped in her tracks. People also usually meant dogs, and these would begin barking as soon as they discovered her. Fortunately, the breeze was blowing away from the encampment, toward her. She was safe. Slowly and carefully, Azeet crept forward. The scent of water was stronger than the scent of people, which meant that they were not together. Azeet veered away from the people smell to the water smell. Her paws began to sink into soft grass and mud. A water hole appeared at her feet. There had to be a can or a bucket near the hole. She found it—a bucket tied to a rope, empty. But around the hole there were small puddles of muddy water. One by one Azeet licked them dry until all had been drained. Time was running out. Azeet made a wide circle, away from the encampment, came back to the gully a safe distance away, and loped on.

Dawn was breaking. Azeet could see its light, reflected from the hillsides ahead, although the gully was still deep in shadow. Azeet quickened her pace. There was still the valley to be crossed, then the river—all to be traveled in broad daylight.

From afar, Azeet spied soldiers atop a hillock. She hid behind a bush and waited for them to move on, but they didn't. Azeet wriggled through the bushes at the foot of the hillock, picking her way carefully to skirt the soldiers. They were scanning the valley through their field glasses, looking for something.

Despite the care she took, as Azeet came around a bend in the gully, one of the soldiers spied the dark fur moving against its yellow bank. He took a quick shot, missed, and before the others could aim, Azeet was gone. Her speed along the winding gully was so great that the soldiers had no clear target; they simply fired at the spot where they had seen her last.

But Azeet knew that she was still in trouble. She was out of the hills at last, but ahead lay the stretch of white dust where she could easily be spotted. To the left lay the well-watered banana plantations. This meant a detour and loss of time, but Azeet's senses told her to head that way. She stayed away from the road and went in the ruts, which partly concealed her as she sped along. Suddenly the sound of a motor overhead came to her ears. The Jordanians had sent up a plane to track Azeet down. Azeet rolled over in the white dust until her brown fur could not be seen from above. The Piper kept going.

But Azeet wasn't the only one who saw the

Piper. The Israeli paratroopers on the other side of the Jordan were alerted by its appearance and immediately reported it to headquarters. The paratroop commander immediately called his officers together. Jordanian planes were never up that early in the morning. This one was clearly looking for someone. Could it be Moishele, the only one missing after the night's raid?

"Get a plane up in the air and have a helicopter ready," the commander ordered. "Put all positions on top alert and warn the artillery. We may have to do a rescue operation. Ask the Air Corps to hold planes in readiness to furnish cover, also to strafe, if necessary. Get going!"

Azeet kept going and had no idea of all these preparations. Ahead of her were the Jordanian positions, waiting, and truckloads of troops were massed along the roads. She could see the banana plantations, closer and closer. Azeet was now streaking across completely level ground, with only a scraggly bush here and there. She had to cross one road to get to the plantations. It was clogged with vehicles. Azeet waited for a break in the line—just a small break, enough to slip through.

The plane was back, above the row of trucks. For a moment the soldiers looked up at the circling plane—and that was enough for Azeet. She hurtled across the road, past the truck wheels. The soldiers saw the streaking fur and fired at the zigzagging figure, but missed. At once the drivers turned their vehicles around and set

off in pursuit. But they overlooked one thing—
the ground around the plantations was so spongy
that the vehicles could hardly make any
headway. Azeet was among the banana trees.

For a moment she stopped. Beyond the plantations were the forward Jordanian positions, separated by gullies which ran right to the Jordan. She
entered one of the gullies, and the scent of the
river ahead sent a quiver of joy through her body.
What she didn't know was that the gully went
right by a Jordanian lookout post, almost at the
water's edge.

The Israeli paratroopers had their field glasses
trained on the lookout post, and suddenly they
saw an object moving along the bottom of the
gully. There was no mistaking the object.
"Azeet!" they yelled. "Azeet!"

"Cover Azeet!" shouted the commander.
"Smoke bombs ready!"

The mortar crew was ready before the words
were out of his mouth. "Six smoke bombs—fire!"

Six streaks of smoke cut through the morning
skies.

The surprised Jordanians couldn't understand
why the Israelis were suddenly firing smoke
bombs. So just to be safe, they retreated from the
lookout point to their artillery position. A dense
cloud of smoke covered the valley. Azeet plunged
gratefully into the smoke and streaked on to
the jungle. A paratroop unit met her there.
Knowing that she was no longer being pursued,
Azeet loped along the bank, plunged into the

water, paddled across the river, and reached the other side, just as her strength gave out. The paratroopers threw her a rope, but Azeet would have none of it. Aching in every muscle, she made it up the bank under her own power, straight into the caressing hands of the paratroopers.

Ori was the first to see the note under the dog's collar. "Fellows, it's from Moishele! He's alive!"

A runner sped away to phone the news to headquarters.

"We'll be using the helicopter again," the commander said when he got the news. "Tonight we'll bring Moishele back."

Azeet was taken to the field kitchen and given a big bowlful of milk. Then she lay down in a corner and waited.

At night the paratroopers boarded the helicopter to rescue Moishele from the prison in Es Salt. Two hours later he was in a hospital in Jerusalem—neatly bandaged and out of danger.

It was against hospital regulations—but there was Azeet, lying happily at the foot of Moishele's bed.

6. THE SNOWS OF MOUNT HERMON

The Hermon mountain range beckons to the Israelis, who are drawn to it with longing and curiosity for the mystery of the unknown. Its very top, at times hidden from view by hovering clouds and fleeting mists, rises to the sky far above its surroundings. It is marked by the shining white snow which covers its broad cap in winter and which, in summer, recedes into its slopes and mysterious crevices.

Israel also has some mountains: the rock-strewn, hallowed mountains of Jerusalem, and the blossoming, green mountains of the Galilee, setting of so much ancient and modern history. The loftiest of them all is Mount Miron, which overlooks the entire Galilee, but it is still no more than half the height of the Hermon.

The mountains of Jerusalem and Safed in the Galilee get snow only for a few hours or days a year at most. But Mount Hermon is covered with snow for months, even years on end. Springs fed by melting snow bubble merrily from its slopes.

The mountain also feeds the Jordan River, and its waters even help make fertile parts of the Negev in the south.

From their settlements in the Huleh Valley and the hills of Manara, the inhabitants of Israel gazed up at the Hermon for many years—but it was beyond their reach. Only the most daring among the young men would go out in the darkness and cross the enemy border to climb the mountain, to follow its trails and, carefully keeping out of sight, to study its wonders and learn about its plants and animal life. From the Hermon they would look out over a vast expanse —the Syrian valleys to the east and the snowy Lebanon range in the west. To the south, laid out like an orderly, colorful checkerboard, were the fields and hamlets of Israel—stretching from the Mediterranean to the Sea of Galilee, the highlands of the Bashan and the Golan, and the cleft of the Jordan Valley, where the silver water coursed between banks of lush green.

The daring young men who returned from the Hermon's snowy crest had many stories to tell about what they had seen. Other young people listened and hoped that some day they, too, might scale those heights. But meanwhile, between Israel and Mount Hermon stood an enemy who not only kept Israelis from enjoying the mountain but also set about bombing and shelling them. The Syrians built fortified positions right into the mountainsides of the Bashan and the Golan and there set up their murderous weapons. In the settlements below, staying underground in the air-raid shelters became part of everyday living.

In 1967, the Syrians prepared for renewed war on Israel, and sent troops to attack the settlements with tank and cannon fire. That was one reason why the Six Day War broke out. But the enemy forces, after all their boasting about their strength, broke and scattered like chaff before the wind when the troops of the Israel Defence Forces came charging at them.

And that was how Israelis were able to return to the crest of Mount Hermon.

The summer of 1967 came and went and winter was upon the mountain. Severe snowstorms swirled about its crest. In a few days it was covered with a fresh white blanket.

One evening, Dr. Harubi was sitting in his home in Jerusalem. Thick pine logs crackled in the fireplace, and a pleasant, fragrant warmth filled the room. Azeet lay stretched out on the rug at her master's feet, napping blissfully. The sound of snapping firewood kept waking her, but all she did was open one eye, which she closed again immediately, in deep contentment.

The radio was on, and over the air came the news about a heavy snowfall in the north—the Hermon slopes and the entire Golan Heights were blanketed with a thick layer. Ski lovers were on their way there for another fling at their favorite winter sport.

Dr. Harubi shifted restlessly in his chair. Pleasant memories of lofty mountains, and soft snow crossed his mind and gave him no peace. Azeet sensed the doctor's restlessness and raised her head. Dr. Harubi looked at his dog. Azeet rose and went over to rub herself against his leg.

Azeet would enjoy the crisp cold mountain air, the doctor thought. After all, her breed came from the snowy lands of Europe—that was why nature had given her such thick, warm fur.

"Miss Azeet Harubi," exclaimed the doctor, jumping up from his chair. "I'm yearning for a feel of the snow. What would you say if I volunteered to be the medic of the army unit on the Hermon? Any objections?"

Azeet looked at Dr. Harubi, as if to say, "The Hermon—in this cold? Come to think of it—that's a good idea. But what about me? Surely you will take me?"

The very next day, Dr. Harubi and Azeet were on their way north.

The military command unit to which Dr. Harubi and Azeet were assigned had its headquarters in the Druse village of Majdal-Shams, the Migdal-Shemesh (Sun Tower) of biblical days. From this village on the lower slopes of the Hermon, a trail runs up the mountain to the very top. The valley to the south is dotted with blossoming orchards of juicy and beautiful apples and pears that are pinkish, as though the frost and the biting wind had pinched their cheeks. Beyond this valley, closed in on all sides, a large placid pool lies in the crater of an extinct volcano. Its pure blue water is cold all year round, and in winter it is glazed with a thin layer of ice. This is Birkat Rom.

To the east there stretches an expanse of rocky hillsides, almost bare of trees. Here the Syrian army has dug in at new positions. Every once in a while a volley of shots and a bursting shell are aimed at Israeli soldiers, and the quiet air is shattered by the warlike sounds. Their thunder rumbles along the Hermon ridges and echoes up the slopes of the Golan Heights.

From time to time the Syrians send units of marauders to attack the new Israeli settlements set up along the empty, yet fertile, stretches of the Golan. The ground, which for years had served as a base for warfare, has again become fruitful and life-giving. The Israelis would not like to see it turn into a wasteland once again. To prevent this, a long string of army outposts guards the new settlements and keeps the marauders and the Syrian army from doing damage there.

When Dr. Harubi and Azeet arrived, everything was coated with a fresh and glistening layer of snow. Boulders and posts, field crops, roads—all were snowed under. Road traffic was at a standstill. The few vehicles which nevertheless were stubborn enough to try to keep going were stalled in the swirling snow. The villagers of Majdal-Shams stayed home; their children drew pictures on the frosted panes or cleaned them to get a better view of the snow.

Only the Israeli soldiers were out, on patrol. Day and night they trudged through the drifts, guarding the border.

Dr. Harubi and Azeet, accompanied by an armed squad, made the rounds of the posts, to teach the men how to take care of their health in the bitter cold. Each post had a heating stove and the men wore cold-weather clothes, but still they had to know what to do in different temperatures, how to act and how to sleep while on long patrol outings, and how to take care of wounds. Dr. Harubi explained all this to the men, while Azeet wagged her tail in agreement, then repeated the rounds to see that his instructions were being followed. He also took care of the soldiers who weren't feeling well and decided whether or not they should be transferred to a hospital.

Azeet loved these rounds. She enjoyed the chance to run and gambol in the thick snow. Chasing the snowflakes as they drifted down lazily from somewhere up above her was a special treat for her.

One evening Dr. Harubi was called to the commander of the unit. "We have been informed," said the commander, "that the Syrians are doing something secretive beyond the northern reaches of the Hermon. They are taking advantage of the low clouds which have settled on its peak and obstruct our lookout points, and we can't get enough information about what is going on there. Tonight, one of our units is going across the Syrian lines and will remain in enemy territory for a few days. Naturally, the men will have communications equipment with them, but I don't want them to run the risk of being spotted by using it too much. The officer in charge of the unit suggests that you and Azeet go with them. Azeet can cross the lines back and forth without arousing suspicion. There are many animals in the mountain, and dog tracks won't stand out. Also, can your dog draw a sled loaded with equipment?"

"Sure thing. That's just the thing for Azeet. I'll love to go along."

"Very good. Everything's set. The unit will leave at nightfall, so that by morning the snow will have covered its tracks completely."

After dusk the column of soldiers, with full gear, set out on its way. In the lead was Azeet, back at her job of warning the soldiers of any enemy forces in the area. She could also pick out a safe path through the snow, avoiding the pitfalls on the way. Azeet was also towing the sled and its load, but the rope which tied her to it was so long that she was able to dart about well ahead of the column. And Dr. Harubi could give her instruction simply by tugging at the rope, with no need of uttering a single word. Arik, the unit commander, trudged at the head of the column, and the men followed in the order of their assignments.

The darkness was very intense—the moon was not due to rise for another two hours. By leaving the base at that time, the unit would cross the

Syrian lines before the moon had made its appearance. Later, the light of the moon would be helpful in finding a suitable spot for a lookout post. But the darkness could also be very tricky; a spot that might look just right in the dark could turn out to be very dangerous in daylight.

The stinging wind pricked the faces of the men like hot needles.

"The devil take it," muttered Nir, in charge of communications. "You'd think it's not enough trouble lugging this instrument on my back, without having this cursed wind blowing in and holding me back. It should at least blow from behind."

Walking behind him, a folded stretcher strapped to his back, Gadi had kindlier thoughts about the wind. "It's our luck that the wind is coming from ahead, where the Syrians are," he said. "This stretcher is rattling a bit, but the wind is taking the sound away, to our rear. Otherwise the Syrians would hear it, and Arik would let me have it worse than the wind is doing."

Dr. Harubi, up ahead with Arik, also liked the way the wind was blowing. "This is just fine," he whispered to the commander. "Thanks to the wind, Azeet will catch the scent of the Syrians a mile away."

Arik nodded and kept his eyes on Azeet's trotting figure. From time to time he also glanced up into the clear, star-studded sky to look for the North Star. This helped him stick to the right route, which he had memorized long before he left the base. He also had a compass, but he was afraid that the instrument wouldn't be accurate because of the metal in the weapons that the men were carrying. Besides, Arik had taken part in so many night marches that checking directions by the North Star was second nature to him.

Azeet went ahead confidently. Every now and then she turned her head, just to make sure that the men and she were going in the same direction. The sled glided smoothly over the snow.

Arik told Dr. Harubi that from now on they had to be extra alert. "I'll tell Azeet," said the doctor. "For this you will have to stop the column for a moment." Arik nodded. Dr. Harubi tugged twice at the rope. Azeet halted at once. Dr. Harubi went up to her, while the men went down on one knee for the brief rest.

Azeet was wagging her tail, swishing it across the snow. Dr. Harubi bent down to her. "Slowly, Azeet. SLOWLY!" he whispered.

The dog snorted to show that she understood. "Slowly" also meant "Be careful!" She did a little dance around Dr. Harubi, to show how pleased she was because he was there, then faced in the direction of the goal.

"Good Azeet," approved the doctor. "Slowly, now. Go!"

The men rose to their feet. "Full alert!" ordered Arik. The words were passed back down the line until they reached the last man—Uri, Arik's deputy. Uri bent forward and whispered to the man in front of him, "Last man has the message." The whisper moved forward until it reached Arik: "Last man has the message."

Arik nodded with satisfaction; despite their trudging in the deep snow, the order had gone back and forth without the men breaking stride. Now he was glad that he hadn't let the men talk him into going easy on such details in training. A hand gripped Arik's arm from the rear and brought him to a halt. Instinctively Arik dropped to one knee. Dr. Harubi was at his side. "Something's up," he whispered, pointing ahead. Azeet had stopped and was sniffing at the ground.

"Mine man, forward!" Arik called. The words went back, each soldier turning his head slightly in relaying them.

Gili, the unit's mine expert, came forward, bending low and taking big steps. In his right hand was his mine-probing knife.

"See if she has anything there that might interest you," Arik said to Gili.

There was nothing on the surface, nor were there any tracks in the clear snow. But Azeet pointed her nose down into the white mass and wouldn't budge. Gili replaced his knife in its sheath and, using both hands, began clearing the snow away from the spot. Azeet eyed him with great interest.

The minutes were ticking away, but Gili worked slowly and carefully. His hands didn't tremble and he went on digging—steadily, easily. His trained fingers were groping about for the object which, if it was there at all, could only be below the surface of the soil.

He found it. Under the layer of snow, buried in

the all but frozen earth, Gili's fingers came in contact with a mine. Azeet's tail began wagging furiously, but before Dr. Harubi could offer her one word of praise, she had already moved a few feet away and her nose was pointed at another mine.

Arik examined the mine which Gili had dug up. "This is an antitank mine," he said. "It's not dangerous for us. We also now know where the rest are, but we can't take the time to dismantle them." He motioned to Gili to replace the mine in the ground. "Cover it up and we'll get going. We can't leave any tracks, in case there's no snowfall."

Azeet didn't understand what Arik was saying, but she intended to stay on the job. Seeing that Arik wasn't interested in the second mine, she scouted around until she found a third.

"Look!" whispered Gili excitedly. "Azeet has shown us the pattern in which the Syrians had laid the mines—in three rows, like in ordinary minefields. This means that the minefield has a fence around it, and we must find it."

Azeet had the answer to that one, too. Having pointed out the third mine—and gotten no action from Gili—she kept looking for something that might attract his attention. When she stopped, there was a low fence strung out in the snow, hugging the ground—a spiderweb fence, which usually hides antipersonnel mines. Anyone who trips this type of fence up can get hurt. Azeet's paws were stepping gingerly between the wires as she moved forward. Dr. Harubi freed her from the sled, and the unit watched her crawl across the area. Her keen nose sniffed no more danger. She was past the minefield.

Arik drew a deep breath of relief. Antipersonnel mines always worried him. He distributed the load aboard the sled among the men. Carefully, they followed one another across the fence, then quickly reloaded the sled and pushed on.

The unit commander glanced at his watch. Soon the moon would rise, and the white expanse of snow would gleam as if it were daylight. The unit was already past the border and the Syrian positions, but the men had to get to the northern slope as quickly as possible. Gili looked at the sky, praying for a snowfall. He and the others had covered up the tracks at the minefield, but a sharp-eyed Syrian patrol passing by the spot would certainly see the difference in the snow. "Where are those clouds?" wondered Gili. "If that snow doesn't come down, the Syrians are bound to find us." Still no clouds came, only absolute stillness and bitter cold.

Dr. Harubi trudged with the others, keeping his head low against the wind. "The Syrians," he was thinking, "are probably sitting tight inside their bunkers, unaware that we are in their territory. Who'd be crazy enough to wander about the Hermon snows at this hour—and in this cold. On the other hand, who knows? They may have spotted us and may be preparing to trap us deep in their territory, and then really let us have it."

The silence was comforting, but also frightening. Nothing could be heard save the sound of shoes crunching in the snow. How could shoes make so much noise? From the east, far on the horizon, came the glow of the rising moon, weak at first but still strong enough to dim the sparkle of the stars. All eyes were on the ball of pale orange rising in the sky—perfectly clear, with no ring around it.

What a wonderful sight! Three deep colors in such sharp contrast—the expanse of white snow, the inky skies in the west and the moon in the east. How beautiful all this would be were it not for the danger! Or was it the danger that was making all this so mysteriously beautiful?

Arik slowed the column down. The men were now at the northern slope, and at this point a suitable hiding place had to be found. The better their observation point, the greater their chances of succeeding in their task. The best place would be a small cleft, hidden from view. Snow drifts are high in the clefts, and it would be a simple matter to carve an igloolike cave out of the piled-up snow. The cleft would have to overlook the northern slope, so that the men might look out at what was going on there without leaving their shelter. Also, thought Arik, this would make it possible for the men to stay together, with no marks in the snow to betray their presence.

Azeet stopped suddenly. The unit had arrived at the slope—but this was as far as it could go. Arik saw that Azeet was standing at the edge of a cliff. Below, the slope stretched down for miles. In the moonlight Arik could make out the folds and the gullies, down to the very foot of the range. The men dropped to their knees; any Syrian looking up from below could easily see dark forms outlined against the moonlit skyline.

Arik studied the cliff. The area to the left looked to be rougher. "Follow me!" he whispered, moving across the ledge. The men, bent over, followed.

Again Azeet stopped. She was at the edge of a pocket which cut across her path. The walls were so steep that no sled could make it.

"Ha!" cried Arik happily. "This is it! Just what we've been looking for. Come close, men." He waited until all his men were bunched around him. "We get into this pocket and cover the top with the tarps we brought along. When the snow comes it will cover the tarp and give us a roof, as in a cave. The opening here will be to the north— exactly according to plan. Okay! Let's get to work."

It took no more than a few minutes to unpack the equipment and supplies from the sled. Supporting poles were put under the tarp to keep it from collapsing under the weight of the snow that would fall on it. Where the pocket opened to the north, the men built a wall of hard-packed snow to narrow the opening down to the width of one man. A person would have to stand very close to it in order to see it at all. Then Dr. Harubi and Azeet settled down near the opening, so that the dog might smell the scent of any approaching enemy.

"And now," said the men to each other as they lay down to sleep, "we should pray for a snowfall. Then this igloo and the tracks we made will be buried under the flakes, and the Syrians won't have the slightest idea that we are here."

Their prayer was granted. Toward midnight, the skies became overcast and snowflakes began coming down, lazily at first, but soon a fresh layer was added to the thick snow blanketing the Hermon range.

"Now I can go to sleep," muttered Arik, and he did so almost before he had fully stretched out.

Azeet lay near Dr. Harubi, but her nose was outside. The clear air there was much better than the stuffy air inside the small igloo.

When the men arose at daybreak, a breathtaking sight met their eyes. The entire lower section of the slope was dark with Syrian soldiers, toiling like ants. Gigantic tractors were shoveling the snow away from the roads, and trucks were unloading enormous crates of equipment. Cement mixers and large cranes kept grinding away to keep the laboring soldiers supplied with concrete.

A light rain was falling and wisps of mist floated across the slope. Through Arik's field glasses, the men could easily see the workers, but whatever they were building was still at too early a stage to reveal what it was going to be. The men were disappointed.

"Never mind," Arik consoled them. "In another day or two, enough of the structure will be up for us to know much more. Anyway, we must report this to Command Headquarters."

He wrote the report out on a sheet of paper—in complicated code, of course. Dr. Harubi folded the paper, placed it under Azeet's collar, and sent her off. The dog returned toward midnight with a reply from Command Headquarters: "You are doing fine. Stay where you are."

The night passed and a new day dawned. The cold grew more intense. The men found it increasingly hard to sit idle. Their bodies were beginning to feel stiff because of the lack of exercise. Under Dr. Harubi's care they worked their limbs sufficiently to keep the blood circulating— they marked time on the spot, swung their arms in all directions, then opened and closed their fists quickly to get the blood to their very fingertips. Every hour, two of the soldiers took turns removing their buddies' shoes and rubbing their toes briskly to keep them from freezing. They also followed Dr. Harubi's advice and took a few gulps of rum, which helps to spread heat throughout the body.

Another day passed. The Syrians stepped up the pace of their labor. Many slabs of concrete were stacked up, and soon the walls of a building began to take shape. Still Arik couldn't make out what it was that the Syrians were putting up.

Could it be an artillery base from which to shell Israeli settlements?

At night Azeet was dispatched with the sled for more supplies. She took another note. As soon as the dog had left, Arik gathered his men for a conference. What more could they do to learn what the Syrians were up to?

"How about kind of stealing up to their camp at night and sort of looking around?" suggested Gili, who was always ready for an adventure.

"And have the Syrians discover our tracks in the morning?" asked Adi, the machine gunner.

"They might even capture us," added Gadi, the orderly. "We don't know their camp layout."

"Okay," said Gili. "What then do we do?"

Silence fell, and all eyes turned to Arik. He was the leader, and the decision was up to him.

"May I propose something?" broke in Dr. Harubi.

"Sure, Doc, go ahead," Arik said.

The doctor made himself more comfortable and lit his pipe. "In the course of the day," he began, "I noticed that some of the Syrians wandered away from the camp—to stretch their legs, I imagine. Some of them came to within a short distance of our igloo, but of course they couldn't see anything from down there, below the ledge. In short, my suggestion is that if one wanders this way again, we kidnap him and bring him here."

"What are you saying?" the men cried in dismay. "You want us to show ourselves in daylight?"

"God forbid," smiled the doctor. "We can't expose ourselves—but Azeet can!"

"Azeet? What can she do?"

The doctor's face sobered. "It's a long shot, but it's worth trying. As one of the Syrians gets near enough to the igloo, we'll send Azeet out toward him. Between her jaws she'll be holding something that would interest most army men—a bottle of liquor, let's say. I'm sure that this will arouse the Syrian's curiosity. He'll want to know where the dog came from and what she's doing here. It'll never occur to him that there might be Israelis around, so that when Azeet leads him to this igloo in the pocket, he'll want to take a peek inside. That's when we'll grab him and ask him a few questions."

"And what do you think the Syrians will do," asked Gadi doubtfully, "when they find that one of their men is missing?"

"They might not notice it until they stop work in the evening," suggested Gili. "They certainly wouldn't go looking for him then, at night, and in the morning they'll figure that he froze to death somewhere, or deserted, and won't take the time from their project to look for him."

Arik sat and said nothing. The doctor's plan was good but dangerous. Still, unless Command Headquarters soon had information about what was going on, the entire country might be facing grave danger. "We'll decide tomorrow, when Azeet gets back," he said finally.

In the meantime, Azeet was making her way

south. The night grew stormy. Snowflakes swirled about her. But the sled, without a load, was light and hardly slowed her down. Besides, the freshly fallen snow had covered all the stones and rough spots, and the sled sped along like a boat on a calm sea. Now that she didn't have to worry about the men, Azeet streaked across the expanse in the crisp air, having a grand time. The snowflakes got into her eyes and tickled her nostrils. As she reached the minefield she slowed her pace and carefully crossed the spiderweb fence so that the sled wouldn't get caught in its mesh.

At Command Headquarters they gave Azeet a bowl of milk, read the note, loaded the sled with food and important equipment parts, covered the load with a white tarp, and sent Azeet off. This time she was accompanied by a missile expert who would have a look at the Syrian works. He followed the dog, tied to her with the long rope and trying hard to keep up with her in the strong wind and whipping flakes.

Suddenly Azeet stopped. The man behind her, plodding on with his head lowered, bumped into the sled and fell into the deep snow. Before he could move, he felt the weight of Azeet's body on his, pinning him down. Having heard from the paratroopers how well trained this dog was, the missile expert offered no resistance. He merely raised his head to the level of the snow and waited for what would come.

He didn't have to wait long. About a hundred feet ahead, five forms emerged from the darkness, moving from right to left. The expert held his breath; this was without doubt a Syrian patrol. Could they have come across the tracks made by Azeet and the sled, earlier, on her way to Headquarters? Perhaps Arik and his unit had been discovered too.

But the Syrian patrol went on without noticing a thing.

Azeet arose, as did the man. Without a word or glance, the two pushed on. It was only when Azeet led the way into the igloo that the expert pounced on her and kissed her eyes and ears, and even her moist nose. Worn out though he was, he related in detail how Azeet had saved him. The men broke into cautious cheers; the story pleased them even more than the fresh food that they received. Azeet was given a double portion, then lay down near Dr. Harubi to rest from her arduous trip.

Arik gave the newcomer all the facts they had been able to gather by watching from their lookout. It was agreed that a final decision would be taken after the missile man had studied the works below for a few hours. This he did at daybreak, peering intensely at the scene down the slope through field glasses, then making notes and drawing sketches of the construction work. Still, he couldn't make up his mind. One thing was certain: Whatever it was, the concrete building—floor and walls—could easily serve as a site for heavy artillery or missiles.

Arik decided to take the chance and follow Dr.

Harubi's suggestion. He told his men to have the equipment and weapons ready.

"If anything goes wrong," he explained, "we might have to move out of here—fast. There won't be a spare minute for anything else." He and the doctor set themselves up at the entrance to the igloo and scanned the slope. Azeet stood nearby. Attached to her collar was a small thermos jug with "coffee" markings. Hami, the bazooka gunner, knew a good deal about the Arabs, and it was he who had reminded Arik that the Moslems do not drink hard liquor, but they do love coffee.

It was already two in the afternoon. Another two hours, and the Syrians would quit for the day. The Israelis knew that it would be better to kidnap a Syrian as late as possible, so that only a little time would be left for his comrades to search for him before dark. But then, it wouldn't do to wait too long. If none of the Syrians came near enough, the whole plan would have to be put off for another full day.

Luck was with them. A Syrian soldier came trudging slowly up the slope, almost staggering under the weight of his winter uniform. As he reached the ledge below the igloo, he stopped and looked about carefully. Then, sure that no human eye was upon him, he undid his belt and laid his rifle aside in the snow. Arik and the doctor turned their eyes away—the Syrian's business was strictly private. . . .

As the soldier was buttoning up his uniform, Dr. Harubi whispered, "Go ahead, Azeet!"

Azeet wriggled out of the igloo and leaped lightly onto the ledge below which the Syrian was standing. Dr. Harubi fed out the long rope tied to the dog's collar but didn't let go of it. Let the Syrian see the rope; he would surely be curious to know what was at the other end. Azeet's step in the snow was so light that the Syrian, gazing out at the slope and enjoying what his eyes were beholding, wasn't aware of the dog's presence until she was right at his side. When he caught sight of the strange animal, he jumped back and almost rolled down the slope. Out of sheer habit he grabbed the rifle and pointed it at Azeet.

"Good God!" muttered Arik, frowning. "We didn't consider the possibility that he might shoot her. The shot will also bring all the Syrians here." He reached inside his jacket and took out a small pistol equipped with a silencer, ready to shoot the Syrian. But as Azeet stood still, her tail wagging in a most friendly fashion, the Syrian got over his scare and lowered the rifle.

Then he saw the thermos jug of coffee. A gift from Allah! The Syrian took a step forward and reached out with his free hand. "Come here, you dog or devil! Come here!"

Azeet stepped back, although her tail went on wagging.

The Syrian edged toward her. "Come, nice dog," he whined. "Come, pretty dog. Let me see what you have there, eh?" His voice changed from honey to vinegar and back again—and all the time he kept drawing nearer and nearer. Arik and the doctor, eyes fixed on Azeet, exchanged grinning glances as they saw how their plan was indeed drawing the breathless Syrian up the slope, to the ledge.

Azeet was now almost at the igloo. To whet the Syrian's curiosity, she made a daring move. With one tremendous leap, she landed right at the entrance—and stopped! The Syrian saw the dark opening. For a moment he paused, staring at it. Then curiosity got the better of him. He didn't suspect a thing.

Azeet backed into the doorway and disappeared from sight. To the Syrian it seemed that the mountain had swallowed her up—thermos jug, rope, and all. "Where are you, devil dog?" he shouted. "I'm tired of chasing you."

Azeet came out and stood facing the Syrian—just an arm's length away. The Syrian made no move. And now Azeet took her last, her decisive step. Keeping her eyes fixed on the Syrian, she retreated partly into the igloo, until only her head remained outside. Still the Syrian made no move. His eyes scanned the cliff. Should he follow that dog through the opening? What was she hiding there? And why was the rope tied to her? Where did the other end lead?

Arik's forehead drew tight with worry. Was the whole plan going to fail at the last moment? Keeping well away from the opening, he glanced at the slope below. The work was going on without letup. No one seemed to have noticed the Syrian's absence. The Syrian, still undecided, shifted nervously from one foot to the other. Arik glanced at Dr. Harubi and nodded. Forward! Dr. Harubi had the same idea. He bent toward Azeet: "Grab him, Azeet!" he whispered. "*Grab* him!"

What happened next was a big surprise to the Syrian. To think that this nice dog with the friendly tail should do a thing like this! For, like a bolt of lightning, without the slightest preparatory move to give her away, Azeet leaped straight at the Syrian's chest, and her jaws clamped tight on the lapel of his heavy coat.

This was where Azeet showed how really clever and well trained she was—had she merely pushed the Syrian backward, he would have tumbled off the ledge, and she with him. This, of course, would have made it impossible for Arik and his men to take him captive and bring him back to the igloo without being seen. Azeet had done the almost impossible. Using the Syrian's body as she would a ball, she bounced off his chest, her paws grabbing the lapel at the same time, then jerked him back with her. He fell forward into the snow at the entrance, and before he could make a move or utter a sound, Arik's viselike fingers had dug into his shoulders and pulled him inside the igloo.

The Syrian was speechless with fright. His body trembled like a leaf. Since he didn't expect any Israelis to be in the area, he was sure that he had fallen into the hands of a band of wicked robbers. It was so dark inside the igloo that he couldn't make out a thing. The sudden change from the dazzling snow outside to the gloom in the igloo had blinded him.

As the Syrian lay there in a daze, breathing heavily, Hami said to him soothingly, in perfect Arabic, "Fear not, O brother, we are not men of evil. We are soldiers of the Israel Defense Forces, and we are here to learn what it is that you are doing. If you tell us, we shall set you free. If you do not, we shall have to hold you as our prisoner. What will happen then to your family?"

"N-no, do not hold me prisoner," cried the Syrian, still trembling. "I shall tell you everything—everything."

"Very good, my brother," said Hami. "You are indeed a man of understanding. In the name of Allah, here! Drink this coffee, and all shall go well with you."

The Syrian reached out eagerly for the thermos jug, then just as quickly drew his hand back.

Hami smiled. "You fear that we might poison you? Not we, my friend—not Israeli soldiers. Look at me as I drink from the same jug." He raised it to his lips and took a deep gulp. "You see? Be not afraid." Hami held the jug out again.

For the first time the fear left the Syrian's eyes. "By Allah," he grinned in relief. "You are indeed fine people. May Allah preserve you." He grasped the jug and drank, deeply at first, then in small gulps, as Arabs do.

The Israelis sat around quietly and studied the Syrian. Could this simple, friendly looking man be the enemy—the Syrian who shells defenseless settlements and talks all the time about wiping Israel off the map?

The soldier seemed to guess their thoughts. "Indeed, I would not have believed it," he said, between sips. "We have always been told: 'Beware of the Israelis! They are murderers and the sons of murderers, and woe is unto him who falls into their hands!' And behold! You have given me coffee! Unbelievable! Everything is in the hands of Allah!"

"That is right," said Hami. "Everything is in the hands of Allah—and we must help him." Everyone laughed, including the Syrian. "There is no Allah but Allah," said the latter fervently, "and Mohammed is his Prophet."

Now that the ice had been broken, Arik motioned to Hami to get on with the questioning.

Soon the mystery was solved. On this slope the Syrians were building a base for ground-to-ground missiles which would rain havoc on all the settlements in the Galilee, up to Safad and Tiberias. The work was to be completed in another two days. The missiles were already on the site and were to be mounted onto the launching pads before the end of the week.

The Israelis were astounded. Only then did they grasp the importance of their mission. Arik went off to one side and, in the beam of the flashlight, prepared a wireless message for Command Headquarters. It contained all the information he had just heard. The news was important enough to risk sending it over the air. Arik called Nir to his side and said,

"As soon as it gets dark, rig up the antenna and

send the message, in code. Mark it 'Urgent and Immediate'; that'll tell them how important it is."

Nir took out his codebook, and in a minute Arik's clear message was translated into the code that made it a jumble of meaningless letters.

The Syrian was seated in a far corner and given a bowl of hot food. Four o'clock was exercise time. Dr. Harubi told the Syrian to get up and work out with the others, to keep his limbs from freezing. It was a funny sight—the Syrian and his Israeli captors exercising together. When he was told to take off his shoes, he was taken aback. Were the Israelis going to make him go barefoot in the snow? But when he saw that they were doing the same, he set about rubbing his toes with great relish, all the time murmuring praise to Allah and his great wonders, beyond the understanding of man. Every now and then he glanced at Azeet. "She is a devil," he muttered admiringly. "How she drew me on—like a woman! Just like a woman, by Allah!"

The others grinned. They were all in a fine mood. The Syrian told about his life in the unit, and the igloo resounded with laughter.

"Quiet," Arik warned his men. "Have you forgotten where we are?"

But no one came to look for the Syrian. The plan had worked perfectly. Darkness fell. Nir went outside and rigged up the antenna. Soon the voice of the wireless operator at Command Headquarters came over the air. Nir transmitted Arik's message and waited for an answer. First the message would be decoded at Headquarters, then receipt of the message itself would be acknowledged.

The men waited tensely. In the darkness all talk died down to a whisper. Finally the awaited reply came: "Nir, Command Headquarters here. Wait for instructions. Over."

The instructions, an hour later, were: "Stay where you are until tomorrow night. You will then receive complete instructions."

That night and the following day passed, and as it did, the tension mounted. Had the Syrians intercepted the message and were now trying to locate the sending station? And what were they planning back at Headquarters? Why should the men in the igloo wait another whole day?

The action began at five in the afternoon: "Nir, Command Headquarters here. Stand by for an important announcement. I repeat—important announcement. Send us a guide."

Arik called the men together. A guide—did that mean that Headquarters had decided to send reinforcements? Okay. Who should go? All the men volunteered.

Azeet alone sat on her haunches, motionless. The men were talking. Well, that was nothing new. Then she saw them looking at her. Aha! Something was in the air, and she rose. After her exploits of the last few nights, all the men felt that she should have the honor to complete the mission. Arik beckoned to her.

"You're the one to go, Azeet. To Command Headquarters. Go, Azeet, go!"

Azeet bounded out of the igloo. Before her

stretched the familiar snow—and now she didn't even have to drag a sled! She sniffed around, found the right direction, and off she streaked, never stopping until she got to Headquarters.

"Azeet!" the commander welcomed her. "So you're the guide they sent! I should have known." He turned to Ruth, at the wireless table. "Tell Niv the guide is here."

Toward midnight, after Azeet had feasted, the commander came up. With him was Niv, the officer in charge of the unit waiting outside.

"Go, Azeet, go! To Dr. Harubi!"

At the mention of her beloved master's name, Azeet's tail began to wag furiously. She ran ahead of Niv, and behind them came the troop, in a long line. Just before dawn, the detachment reached the igloo.

"It's unbelievable," said Niv to Arik. "She led us straight, like a magnet. She's one for the books. Didn't stop or lose her bearings even once. I tell you, she's out of this world."

Dr. Harubi grinned happily.

A voice came over the air, followed by a message in code. Nir decoded it quickly, and his heart began beating faster. This is what it said: "Air Corps will attack missile base at dawn. Immediately after attack, you are to take advantage of the confusion to swoop down on the base and capture missile parts and any other important equipment. Helicopters will come in under air cover and pick you up along with the materials. Over!"

The men broke out into cheers and began readying their gear. Niv called his unit together and outlined the plan of action. Arik wanted his men to be in on the action, too.

"Nothing doing," said Niv flatly. "You fellows have done your share."

"Nothing doing nothing," insisted Arik. "You want us to sit here and look on while you fellows carry out the action? You don't know us very well, do you?"

"Okay, fine." Niv gave in. "You come with us. What about Azeet?"

"Don't worry about Azeet," Dr. Harubi smiled. "The Syrians will run faster when they hear her barking than when they see you coming. Ever hear her launch an attack?"

"Good, good." Again Niv yielded. "Who can argue with Azeet?"

Hami placed some food by the Syrian's side and told him what was going to happen. "Remember," he warned. "Do not leave the cave while the bombardment is on, lest evil befall you. But once we are gone, you will be free to return to your home. And remember, always—the Israelis are humans. They, too, are the children of Al-mighty Allah."

"Everything is from Allah," replied the Syrian fervently, shaking hands with Hami. "You are indeed children of Allah, and he will safeguard you from all harm!"

The roar of jet planes broke from the skies, and the first wave of the Israeli Air Corps came knifing through the clouds. The thunder of exploding bombs shook the Hermon range. From the pile of missiles, smoke mushroomed upward, then settled on the blackened snow. The men of the Israeli units came charging down the slope at the milling Syrians.

"Beat it!" the Israelis yelled at the Syrians, as the latter raised their hands high. "We have no time for prisoners. Go home!"

As one unit gathered up the missile parts and the radar equipment, others prepared the landing field for the helicopters, lighting smoke candles to mark the field and the direction of the wind. On the face of the Hermon, looking as if they were skiing down the slope, came three large helicopters. Arik fired a rocket into the air—the signal for permission to land.

"Line up on two sides," ordered Niv, and the men grouped as he directed. As soon as the helicopter's rails touched the snow, they yanked open the doors, loaded the material, and climbed aboard. The helicopters took off.

"Make a turn over there," Arik said to Opher, the pilot of the lead helicopter, pointing toward the igloo. "I want to see what's with the Syrian."

Sure enough, there he was, at the entrance, his arms filled with food parcels. Opher brought the helicopter close, and the men inside waved good-bye to the Syrian. Azeet wagged her tail.

"*Maa salaameh.* Good-bye in peace," said Hami.

The Syrian looked at the smoking ruins below

him and kept waving at the disappearing helicopters. He was very confused. "*Wallah*, a crazy world, truly a crazy world. Everything is best left in the hands of Allah!"

Temple Israel
Minneapolis, Minnesota

IN MEMORY OF
ELAINE SIMON
FROM
ESTELLE ¢ PHIL GROSSMAN